Wolf's Temptation

Elizabeth Lapthorne

ELLORA'S CAVE
ROMANTICA®
WWW.ELLORASCAVE.COM

CHASING LOVE

Christiana Rutledge has finally graduated from college and is ready to head back home and help her father run Rutledge Securities and lead the Pack. But first, she has to attend the Graduation Ball.

After working for hours on just the right costume, she can turn herself into the alluring, seductive woman she knows is inside herself. For one night, she will cast off all her inhibitions and let loose. Then she can move on to her responsibilities to the Pack and her family. And perhaps meet her True One, her mate for eternity.

Edward Matthews couldn't believe the lengths he was going to for a night with Christiana. Growing up together, she had offered her childish heart to him. Youth he had been, he had rejected her and regretted it for years. Crashing her masked ball and seducing Christiana might be one way to get his no-strings-attached affair with Christiana. Or at least work her out of his system! Maybe after a few days of hot, sweaty sex they could both get on with their lives.

What neither realizes is that they are actually chasing each other. And Chasing Love.

TWIN TEMPTATIONS

Samantha Monique Rutledge is happy with her life. She has her work as a PI, an extended family whom she adores and a twin brother blissfully in love. After being introduced to Callum MacLennon, who is about to leave for a long-term project in Australia, Sam willingly gives in to temptation and indulges in what she believes will be one night of raunchy, make-her-scream sex with no strings, no lingering emotions and certainly no complications.

Eight months later, Sam still can't get the delectable man out of her mind. Not only has Callum returned, but two little wolf cubs have gone missing, and her twin brother Alexander wants her to discreetly investigate whether her one-time lover had anything to do with it. Balancing herself between the twin temptations of finding the lost cubs and indulging herself in her lover, however, is harder than she could have believed — especially since Callum is making it crystal clear that he's all for them giving in to temptation and solving this puzzle together, *intimately.*

An Ellora's Cave Publication

www.ellorascave.com

Wolf's Temptation

ISBN 9781419964473
ALL RIGHTS RESERVED.
Chasing Love Copyright © 2004 Elizabeth Lapthorne
Twin Temptations Copyright © 2008 Elizabeth Lapthorne
Edited by Martha Punches and Sue-Ellen Gower.
Cover art by Syneca.

Trade paperback publication 2011

WOLF'S TEMPTATION

Elizabeth Lapthorne

෨

CHASING LOVE

TWIN TEMPTATIONS

CHASING LOVE

ജ

Trademarks Acknowledgement

Prologue

ஐ

Christiana sat beside her grandfather's bedside, determined by her sheer will alone not to let him die. For once she wasn't squirming, eager and full of energy to run outside in the sunshine. Maybe Edward and her parents were right, maybe she was finally beginning to grow up.

Her parents and all three sets of her aunts and uncles were having a powwow in the back kitchen, talking quietly and sipping their eighth, or maybe tenth, pot of coffee and herbal tea of the day.

No one knew Christiana was in here with her Grampa and, if they did, her dad would get that *look* on his face, the one that indicated death would be a preferable alternative to his anger.

The thought made Christiana smile. Her dad was a piece of cake. Her mom, on the other hand, would make her wash all the pots and pans from dinner, poking her dad in the stomach until he agreed and pointed in the direction of the sink.

Yech.

Christiana felt a snicker escape her. With her vivid imagination, she could just *see* the scene unfold before her eyes.

She swallowed the snicker quickly when she noticed her grandfather had finally opened one eye. She smiled, radiant in her happiness. When her grandfather gave her a much weaker version of his usual happy-go-lucky smile, she felt immense relief as the innate knowledge she took for granted now washed over her.

Her grandfather would be just fine.

"Thought you were Naomi there for a moment, child. Snickering away at me and my old thoughts. She must have left just before you snuck in here."

When one old eye cracked open toward the half-open window letting in a warm breeze to freshen the room, Christiana felt surprised with the strength of his next comment.

"What the hell are you doing on a bright, sunny day like today, stuck indoors with an old codger like me?"

Christiana smiled hugely, her fourteen-year-old world suddenly righted once more.

"Oh, just sitting, Grampa. I'll go outside and play in a minute. Are you feeling okay?"

The Old Man sighed and rubbed his wrinkled old hand along Christiana's much smoother and smaller one.

"I'll be fine, child. Naomi kicked my ass good and strong. I'm going to be hanging around for a while longer, it seems. Lovely to see she's still got a temper on her. Wouldn't be my Naomi if she weren't kicking my ass and ordering me about."

The harsh words were said softly, reverently, and Christiana knew her grampa missed his True Mate more than anyone could ever understand. Yet something about the strong, beautiful, long-dead woman touched her deeply. Christiana felt a kinship with her that no one else, with the possible exception of Edward, could really understand.

Sometimes Christiana could *feel* the older woman around her, helping her make decisions and pushing her on the right path, much like her mother would when she was about to steal a cookie from the jar or cheat in a game of cards with her siblings.

It was strange but something about this whole situation led her to believe that her Grandfather might understand how she felt and give her some advice.

"Grampa," she began. When the tired eyes opened, she felt almost bad for interrupting him. He had been so sick all week; he really needed his rest. When she frowned and squeezed his hand, the Old Man smiled and patted her hand again.

"I'm sticking around this time, my love. Naomi would make life, or maybe death, miserable if I left right now."

Christiana nodded. She really shouldn't bother her grandfather right now. Maybe later. She felt surprised when he continued.

"Go talk to Edward, sweetest. He'll be the one to help you through all your troubles."

Christiana felt a spurt of surprise. It was a well-known secret that her grandfather thought she and Edward were True Mates. For years she and Edward had teased each other about it, not paying too much attention to what the future held. Yet now, after having seen truly for herself that her dearly loved Grandfather wouldn't stay around to help her all her life, she wondered if all his joking was just camouflage for the truth.

"Edward? But..."

The Old Man laughed without even opening his eyes. "Of course sweetest. Whom do you turn to, to organize those cookie and chocolate chip raiding exercises of yours?"

Christiana felt a flare of surprise. *How did he know about those?*

"And who do you tease and taunt mercilessly when he brings home some poor, unsuspecting girl and who manages to drive them off, usually within the hour?"

Christiana felt her face flush. *Surely everyone didn't know about that? She'd been particularly careful after the debacle of the first girlfriend crying to all and sundry about being pushed into a convenient mud puddle.*

"And who would you do anything at all for, who is the man you've had a crush on since the first moment you can recall?"

Christiana bit her lip and tried to think. Was this what her dad had meant when he explained that in the following couple of years, her early teenage years, she would really start her road to becoming a woman?

At the time she had laughed and informed him that she had learned all about women's menstrual cycles back in fifth grade. She smiled when she remembered how he had turned bright, bright red and rushed off to her mom complaining loudly that *no one* should be fool enough to have daughters. Her uncles had jeered at him until she had rushed to defend him. The memory had been all but forgotten.

Until now.

Was she supposed to organize Edward now? Kick him up the ass like Naomi did for Grampa when he got too tired?

Patting her grandfather's hand, Christiana stood up, kissed him on the cheek and left the room.

It was time she became a woman.

* * * * *

"...so you see, Edward, I think we should start dating and then organize to get engaged."

Christiana smiled at herself. Really this whole growing up thing wasn't anywhere near as hard as all her friends at school complained about! A little thought and some firm but friendly action and everything ended up perfectly!

Edward had been still as a stone as she had explained her reasonings behind why they should get together. She couldn't, of course, tell him her *real* reasons. One of her girlfriends from school, Danni, insisted that men ran a mile when you confessed you loved them to distraction and doodled their names on everyone's pencil cases.

So she had been very logical, very *masculine* she prided herself, and explained all her logical, non-love-related reasons for their dating and marriage. She explained how they had known each other forever and they got along really well together as buddies.

14

Then she moved on to explain how it made perfect sense for them to not only start dating, but get married as well because their parents already knew each other and liked one another just fine. None of those mother-in-law from hell or monster-in-law stories for *them!*

She finally shut her mouth. She had to be a tiny bit nervous as she was starting to babble.

Calmly, she waited for Edward to agree with her. She frowned a little as she pondered what they should do first. Does one kiss one's "boyfriend" when they first start dating or do they wait a while?

Never having had a real boyfriend — Tommy back in second grade didn't count as they had only held hands for two days before he left her for Susie in third grade — she wondered if maybe she should have organized a few trial runs first to get the basics of dating down.

Shaking her head, Christiana instantly changed her mind. No, she wanted to experience everything fresh and new with Edward. She was doing the right thing.

"You know, Christi-girl, I think you must be a little tired. What say you go and have a nap?"

Christiana felt her face flush. A *nap?*

What was she, some two-year-old?

"Don't be stupid, Edward. I'm telling you we should start dating, with a view to getting engaged when I turn sixteen. Or maybe eighteen if you're feeling *scared.*" There! A little taunting should make him come up to scratch.

Edward was shaking his head in that condescending manner he had picked up from one of his floozy ex-girlfriends. She *hated* it when he did that to her.

Without even paying attention, she felt her hands rest on her hips, much the way her mother's would when she was about to let loose a tirade on her father. Strange how she had never noticed the mannerisms of her parents she had picked up unconsciously.

"Are you turning me *down?*"

Edward sighed.

"I don't think either one of us is ready, Christi-girl. You're only fourteen for heaven's sake." He held up a hand placatingly, angering her even more. "Sure, you're *nearly* a woman but, really, you're still just a little kid. You have no idea what you're doing or where you're going. While *I* am looking forward to heading off to college and have no intention of tying myself to a little girl whom I'll only be seeing twice a year. At Easter and Christmas."

Christiana felt her face flame a bright red. She reassured herself she was angry but the tears she was forcing away, so Edward would never see or guess, made her inner soul ache with disgust.

So Edward didn't want to *tie* himself to her?

She'd show him. It was obviously well past the time she should get over her crush on the beast. Time she worked out her own life's plans. If Edward didn't want to be a part of them, fine. He could be her *buddy*, she scorned at the word.

Sure, she'd stay buddies with him, tell him her deeds and secrets, but never, never, *ever* again her thoughts of the heart. No sense on wasting that sort of time and emotion on the stupid jerk.

Christiana stormed off without another word. She didn't think she could bear hearing one more of his words on the subject. *He* might think she was still a child but her emotions had suddenly matured over the last few hours. She couldn't explain it and refused to even try to put it into words to a man who obviously thought she was simply an annoying kid.

She ran to her favorite tree in the woods and climbed as high as she could, higher than she ever had before. As she climbed, her mind spun with thoughts, decisions and plans.

The plan of tarring and feathering Edward while he slept, although cheering her up immensely, was thrown out for practical reasons. Her mother would not only ground her for a month, but would possibly spank her for the first time in more years than she could count.

Going to her father and uncle's and asking for help with her revenge was also out. They would help her, had sworn black and blue to beat the crap out of any man who hurt her. But she not only couldn't do that to the beast, even though he deserved it, but she wanted to work this out herself. She was a *woman* now, she needed to learn how to do things on her own.

She had a knack for people, or *most* people anyway, people with a brain and sound reasoning, not *men* on the cusp of heading off to the all-important *college*. She had a vague interest in the Pack's businesses. Maybe she should talk to her dad about that.

Her musings and impulsive decision-making lasted until she flopped down on the highest branch that would hold her weight. She had climbed so high the ground was obscured. Her mother would have kittens if she found her.

Christiana sighed and tried to fight the tears. Not even the thought of her mother having kittens could cheer her out of this mood.

But Christiana needed some time to recover and, she felt sure as the tears dripped down her face, to bawl her eyes out and face the world with a smiling face later.

Christiana cried and cried. Finally hiccupping away the last of her tears, she mentally began to prepare herself.

So the jerk didn't want to tie himself down? That would be fine. She could still tease him and taunt him. Still make him miserable and embarrassed to bring any woman back home with him. Yet it was time to get on with her life. No more mooning over *him*, no more dogging his footsteps or scrawling his name on every sheet of paper she wrote on.

No more.

Christiana was organizing her own life and this new life had Edward Matthews firmly in the position of a friend, a *buddy*, and not her True Mate.

Smiling, Christiana wiped away the last of her tears. She would get hugs and cuddles from her dad and uncles when she returned. That would solve all her sad feelings. It always had and probably always would.

And then she would start her new life as a new woman.

A woman who absolutely, *positively* was *NOT* in love with the beast Edward Matthews.

Chapter One
Ten years later

ை

Christiana touched her peacock-blue satin mask once more—just to make sure it was still in place. She looked out over the huge, extremely crowded ballroom and smiled. It was just after finals and there was a definite air of "party" among the graduates.

A vast proportion of the college had turned out to celebrate. All the different departments were represented at the end-of-year ball. The French doors were thrown wide in the vain attempt to alleviate some of the heat. It wasn't particularly effective, as thousands of milling ex-students drinking, dancing and generally having a blast created even more heat.

Christiana opened her matching peacock-blue fan and tried to create some semblance of a breeze. She had made her gown herself and she was particularly proud of it.

Off the shoulder, with a corset-style bodice and a flowing, elegant skirt, the material was the same color silk as her mask and fan. It had only taken the entire two weeks since her graduation ceremony to sew it. She had slaved every night and most of her days to get it just right.

The last two weeks had been painful, but informative. There had been more mistakes and things she had learned than most of her college years had given her.

Pricking her fingers, breaking the sewing machine needles, and much swearing was only the beginning. Also involved were over a dozen phone calls back home to her mom for instructions on how to re-thread the needle, cut "with the grain" and other silly tidbits of information the sewing instructions. Whoever assumed a novice would understand all this?

Blood, sweat, tears and tantrums aside, the final product gave no indication of the immense effort she had put forth for her Graduation Ball.

Still, the final product was nothing to be sneezed at and she felt like a million dollars amongst the glittering crowd. She sipped her cola, determined to hold onto the can she had snagged from an unwary tuxedo-clad waiter. She had no desire to get drunk and end up rolling around on the grassy lawns outside with some masked stranger.

Many of the men present wore the traditional tux and mask but some had at least made a token effort for the masquerade. There were men in togas, football heroes, complete with helmets instead of masks, leather-clad bikers and other assorted costumes. Christiana had recognized a large number of the men and women present, held a few "congratulations-aren't-you-glad-we-made-it?" conversations. But by and large, she felt at loose ends.

She had danced most of the night away and was glad to rest her aching feet, yet she wasn't quite ready to pack up her gear and head on home. Her business degree would come in great use to help lead her Pack into its future, yet she was still young, she had only just turned twenty-four.

Working part-time, stretching the fourth year of her degree into two by studying part-time, she had learned some of the fundamentals of her father's wide-ranging business. It made her feel far more confident to be entering the ranks of her father's employees with *some* working knowledge of how the business ran.

Even so, she didn't know *where* in the business she wanted to fit herself—or indeed even *if* she wanted to spend the rest of her life working in this business.

She wanted to live a little more before trying to find a mate—*groan*—and committing herself to learning the ropes of leadership from her dad.

Sure, she had dragged her feet these last two years—playing at being the student and getting a very ground-level look at the business...but somehow Christiana couldn't help but wonder if there weren't *more* to life than her college and work.

She had no desire to escape her fate, yet was this all there was to life? What happened to the romance? The excitement? The daring games and pranks she had enjoyed pulling with her roommates?

Scouting the crowd, she located Maggie, her roommate. Christiana had to smile as she located her over in the corner, practically having sex in the darkened alcove. Even from clear across the room Christiana could see both of their tongues diving and hands groping. She shook her head at her much-loved roommate's antics.

Maggie had confided her plans of getting pregnant, marrying her partner and setting up a home-based business. Christiana found it highly ironic that this less-than-pure feminist friend's plan would actually use her damned degree *more* than most of the people present in this room.

Strange how, for every step forward women made, they seemed to take another three steps backward.

Sighing, she looked away from the madly kissing and groping couple and sipped her cola again. She loved Maggie to bits but she was determined to live some of her life before she truly settled down. College had been fun but she had worked hard to earn her degree. She hadn't had enough of a taste of adventure and romance to settle her just yet.

Maggie was looking forward to returning home, to organizing a huge white wedding and buying the proverbial white picket fenced home and having three-point something children. Yet, Christiana itched for something *more*. She had no idea what more was but it wasn't to return home to her family's not-so-veiled hints at marrying Edward!

She loved Edward, really she did, but how could one marry the boy one grew up with? She and Edward had been as close as close could be for most of their lives. She had tried her teenage seduction skills out on him — failing miserably — and had afterwards resolved to truly save herself for her True Mate, someone who would not only understand her pathetic attempts at seduction, but also appreciate her and her saved virginity.

Her father and uncles had no problems with her attitude but, strangely enough, they didn't really understand her philosophy either. Yet who were they to argue with keeping their eldest daughter/niece chaste? Certainly not them!

It had been hard — she simply *burned* with lust at times — yet a smart worldly woman knew the power of Ebay and online shopping and could get any number of toys and manuals and learn how to satisfy oneself without breaking the all-important hymen.

But somehow, in her self-explorations and desire to graduate with honors, she had missed something important. Men around college would only go so far with a woman who flat-out refused sex — and wasn't afraid of saying so up front.

Soon it was well-known she was a great *buddy* — how she hated that word — a kick-ass date to the football, as long as *her* team won, and generally a great pal. You just couldn't push her into bed or ask for more than a casual groping session. So she found herself either treated as one of the boys or, worse, like a kid sister.

And so she had missed huge chunks of the romance a budding relationship could offer, the daring and adventuring her still-young soul craved.

Stupidly, she had thought tonight would be different. She would dress up, dress alluringly, be masked so no one would know who she was. She could flirt and play and tease and explore that more mysterious side to romance she had been missing.

The sexual side of things, she knew as well as any virgin possibly could. But the romance and mystery, that getting-to-know you flirting side of relationships, she had missed, and damned if she would return home to her responsibilities without a taste of romance and adventure!

Christiana finished her cola and put the can down on a nearby table. She resisted the urge to pace. Pacing in these stilettos and long gown would undoubtedly end up with her flat on her face making a fool of herself. Sighing in resignation, she saw Benjamin,one of her management buddies. Maybe she should get back out onto the dance floor.

While romance and passion might *still* be missing tonight, she could nevertheless enjoy herself being swept around the dance floor by a good friend.

"Excuse me," a deep, husky, masculine voice interrupted her internal monologue, "but may I request this dance?"

Frowning, Christiana realized she didn't immediately recognize whose voice it was. Turning around, she looked up—a rare enough occurrence, being naturally five-foot-nine and tonight wearing three-inch stilettos—to be grinned at boldly by a masked pirate of all things!

A blue bandana held back what looked to be wild, black curls. A black silky looking mask obscured the rest of his face down to his chin. A few days' worth of growth was stubbled around the chin, so she couldn't get any indication of what his face looked like. His eyes were dark brown, a deep, rich, lovely color that drew on something inside her.

She shook her head and smiled She was becoming fanciful!

"Do pirates request?" she teased, happy one of her friends had dressed up enough so that she couldn't immediately identify him. Guessing who he was would be fun for the rest of the dance.

She laughed outright as she felt herself swept up into large, strong arms and half-carried out to the dance floor where lots of people milled, about to start the next dance.

"Excellent point," her pirate granted. "Pirates steal and pillage, pirates do not politely request dances from fair maidens."

Gurgling her laughter, Christiana was happy when a waltz was struck up. Any excuse to be dragged against this large pirate's chest was welcome. While she had never been the snuggling type, allowing herself to be brought against his muscled body and led around the crowded dance floor seemed to be the perfect start to the rest of the evening.

Christiana closed her eyes and committed the sounds and feelings to memory. *This* was what she yearned for, for an unknown pirate to sweep her off her feet and carry her off into the distance.

"Are you falling asleep on me?" the pirate laughed.

"No," she replied seriously, "I'm committing this to memory."

"Ah, I thought fair damsels screamed and fainted when taken away by pirates."

Christiana snorted. "Maybe stupid maidens do. *I* think it's fantastic and romantic. Why waste such a spectacular fantasy by fainting dead away when one can wallow in the romance?"

"Ahh, a bold young thing."

Christiana frowned. She wasn't particularly young. Most everyone present was her age or only a year or two younger, depending on how fast they had moved through their four years of college. What an odd thing for one of her classmates to say. She looked back up to her pirate and tried to figure out which friend he was.

He looked slightly familiar but, as she ran through the guys she sat next to during lectures and labs, no one sprang to mind. Frowning, she tried to figure out if he was the partner of one of her girlfriends.

"Such a sad frown marring your fair skin," he murmured, stroking a finger down her forehead, trying to push away her frown. Christiana was surprised to feel a ripple of electricity at the touch. She started feeling worried and excited at the same time, a very rare occurrence for her.

"Who are you?" she finally caved in and asked. "You seem...familiar...but I can't put my finger on where I've met you. You're not Talia's new partner, are you? Because I've heard he's a bit of a good-looking stud, but a total ladies' man, and I don't help partners of my friends cheat."

Her pirate merely pulled her closer and swung her in the opposite direction as the key changed, indicating the end of the song was near.

"I know who you are, Sweet One, and that's all that really matters."

The endearment rang bells in the back of her head. Christiana was surprised to find her mouth going dry. What was it about this man?

He looked handsome, from what little she could glean through his costume, but her body seemed to be reacting with a startling amount of desire, with very little provocation. The intensity of her sexual response to this masked man simultaneously confused and excited her.

Maybe she needed to get laid more than she realized. Smiling at herself, she made a mental note. Time for new batteries.

Her pirate swung them around in a different direction, so they cut a swath through the crowded ballroom. Many couples were grouped in the shadows of the room, the night's darkness being allowed in through the candlelight and opened French doors.

Everything added up to the romance and passion her soul had craved for years, yet there was still something niggling at the back of her mind. This reaction from her body seemed heightened for some reason. She wasn't blind, nor had she cloistered herself away for the last ten years.

Christiana knew how she reacted when she saw a stud, when a handsome man would run his eye over her curves and smile in appreciation. So, too, did she know how her heart beat faster on the rare occasion she would go out on dates, or make out in the back of a movie theatre.

Her heartbeat certainly felt accelerated but the thumping of her heart, her shortness of breath, wasn't due to the exertion of dancing. It seemed to be related to the electricity between her and her pirate.

Christiana frowned, not at all sure she understood what was going on. Her gut was telling her there was more to this pirate than she fully understood. He certainly knew who she was, yet she simply for the life of her couldn't put her finger on which particular friend or tutorial buddy he was.

Her damned pirate totally held the upper hand, both in this dance as well as the whole encounter, and it irked her even as she felt herself growing warm and excited. The first flush of sexual curiosity and desire seeped into her system like a drug, making her want to rest back in her pirate's arms and let him take her away.

Whoa! her mind cried out and Christiana frowned even more. Fainting maidens and submissively tame fantasies were not her. She had been in control of herself and determined to make her own destiny since she was a teenager.

So why the sudden desire to give everything over to some strange masked man?

As the music wound to a halt, she prepared herself to fob him off to one of her colleagues with a promised dance. Her mind was creating problems where there undoubtedly were none and her mixed emotions, mingled with her burgeoning sexual curiosity and hunger, were making her unable to think clearly.

She needed a breather, another cola or maybe some coffee. Anything to clear her head and take a step back for a moment.

Yet, he didn't relinquish his grip.

"Let's get some fresh air," he laughed as he led her out the French doors they had halted beside.

Before she could decide whether to protest or indulge in the long-held fantasy of a strong man taking command of her, her huge, masked pirate was spiriting her away into the enormous college gardens and out into the moonlit night.

So much for being in charge of her own destiny! Christiana smiled and allowed herself to be led meekly away, all the while plotting furiously and arguing with herself on what she should be doing.

Her soul eventually won out. She had wanted passion and mystery, romance and excitement, and here he was leading her outside the crowded ballroom and into the moonlit night.

*Be careful what you wish for...*she intoned silently to herself.

Smiling, she allowed Fate to lead her away in the guise of one huge, masked pirate.

Chapter Two

စာ

Edward tried his damndest to keep not only his hands from roving, but his laughter contained.

Just before she had left to return to college last Christmas, she had turned down his offer, *again*, saying she couldn't possibly become intimate with someone she had known *forever*.

Damn her.

It wasn't like he was asking her to marry him, or shackle herself to him for eternity. He simply wanted a no-strings-attached affair. A mutually satisfying fucking frenzy between two very old friends. A weeklong orgy where he could get her out of his system and stop comparing every fricking woman he met to her.

She wanted passion and romance? She wanted some huge stranger to sweep her off her feet? When Sophie, Christiana's mother, had laughingly confided to him some of her antics while she tried to sew her own costume for the Graduation Ball, he had thought of the perfect solution.

Romance her, sweep her off her feet, carry her into the night and seduce her senseless. Finally get her out of his system and move on with his life. Find his True Mate and live in peace.

He had almost forgotten how delicious her scent was or maybe he had deluded himself into believing his memories were exaggerated. Either way it didn't help his light-headedness at the nearness of her delectable body and delicious scent.

Among the crowded, sweaty and drunken masses she was a breath of fresh air. She filled his lungs with her delicate scent and he feared he would drown in her.

As he led her around the back, to a secluded spot where he couldn't scent any of the other young adults rutting away like animals in heat, he drew Christiana up to him. Enjoying the feel of her body pressed along his, he tried in vain to stop his cock from becoming iron-hard.

Giving in to temptation, he bent down to kiss her.

Her lips softened deliciously and he swallowed his groan of desire. Despite the fact they had known each other their whole lives, Edward had only kissed Christiana a handful of times. Over half of those kisses had occurred before the age of ten for him, and seven for her. As he was now twenty-seven years old, the fact he could recall these incidents in accurate, fairly intimate detail sometimes slightly worried him.

Her scent enveloped him and he drew her closer, wanting to crawl inside her skin. This woman had been his playmate and confident for most of his life. Even though they argued and often fought like cats and dogs, he knew in a crunch he could trust her with his life. In his mind, that counted for a hell of a lot.

And now he was seducing her. Weird but true.

He had always figured the openness and honesty that lay between them could extend naturally to the bedroom. They had precious few secrets, had always refused to let the ordinary male/female barriers come between them.

He had held her when she had been twelve and bawling over her first period. She had teased him mercilessly when he had brought his first serious girlfriend back to meet his family and her own. He still cringed at the open and child-like innocent questions she had asked him when he got his first teenage boner in her presence.

He had thought that their sexual curiosity could be taken care of just as simply and in their usual straightforward manner.

But no, he had royally screwed that up over ten years ago. At the idiotic age of seventeen, Christiana had been just fourteen and had proposed they date and get engaged. Her grandfather had been seriously ill and, even though the Old Man hadn't pushed them exactly, his wishes for them were known by every member of both their families.

Worried sick about the man he considered his grandfather and topped off with the burning urgency to go and sow his wild oats most seventeen-year-old men had, he had politely, but firmly, spurned Christiana.

She had never mentioned sex with *him* again. They talked about sex and positions and manners like normal friends, and what sometimes all their talking felt like they discussed it *ad nauseum*. By the time the four years of his college education had passed and he had moved back home to settle down, he had begun to understand just how important Christiana felt to him.

It took him a while to understand but he measured each and every woman he became involved with against her and most came up depressingly short.

By the time she had been eighteen and beginning college herself, he had been broaching the issue of sex between them. He smiled sardonically as he recalled just how firmly-but-politely she had squashed the conversation each and every time he had brought it up since then. It almost felt as if Fate or the Goddess was laughing at him through the younger girl.

That must account for the raging boner straining his pirate's breeches. Or for the heart pounding fearfully fast in his chest, acting as if it were about to burst out of his chest cavity. Or the incredible, animal lust he had for this delicate woman.

She wanted romance and passion, he reminded himself, not for a raving lunatic to strip her bare on the college lawns and fuck her senseless here and now. Romance and mystery would be perfect to pique her interest and then leave her wanting more. Even better would be if he could stay masked long enough that she wouldn't know who he was. *That* was mystery and romance.

Sighing at the idiotic notions females sometimes came up with, Edward tried to rein in his hunger. He had lusted over Christiana for the best part of ten years; he could wait a few more nights while he seduced the woman. She had waited years for him — he could still tell she was a virgin. He didn't understand how but he *knew* he would be able to tell when she gave herself to another man. He could try to wait a couple of nights for her.

Maybe three at the most.

His intentions had become pure over the last minute but everything flew out of the window as Christiana moaned in hungry lust and opened her mouth for him.

How could any man resist that invitation?

Without even thinking about it, Edward bent her back into the tree and thrust his tongue into her mouth. *He* would have been gentlemanly about this kiss but, if *she* was going to invite him inside, who the hell was he to turn her down?

Stroking inside her mouth, tasting her damp, inner flesh, Edward was surprised to find his knees beginning to buckle. Straightening his stance, he decided to hell with chivalry. Chivalry never satisfied good old lust. Pressing his erection between her legs, he swallowed her gasp, and then drank her moan of approval like the sweetest of nectars.

Twining with her tongue, dancing inside her body, Edward felt almost lightheaded from the lack of blood to his brain. Everything had headed south and congregated for a party in his pants.

He squashed the thought that *never* had he felt such driving, forceful lust before. Never had he wallowed so lazily in a woman's scent before.

When Christiana reached down to touch his burning shaft, he struggled to remember why he wasn't planning on stripping her and fucking her here. Taking a deep breath, he tried to come to his senses.

Chapter Three

✍

Christiana touched her pirate's rock-hard erection and barely suppressed a moan. She didn't know who he was and she didn't care. He smelled of home, of the woods back behind her parents' enormous house, of salty masculinity and some other elusive factor she simply put aside to his unique scent.

She had never touched an erect male cock flesh-on-flesh before but, boy, she felt tempted. She didn't know if it had anything to do with the night, the moonlight shining down on them, or even this mystery pirate of hers but something inside her screamed for some release and sexual playing.

Even through the thin, shiny breeches, she could feel the heat *radiating* from his cock. As she touched it, it seemed a curious mixture of hard and soft. She had talked at length with Maggie and a few other close girlfriends about men's cocks, their varying sizes and shapes.

It might be the virgin in her but this man seemed larger than most she had been warned about. She felt a giggle bubble inside her as she mentally tried to measure his length.

She had a 'special' ruler back in her dorm. One night, she and Maggie had drunk an entire bottle of red wine and laughed themselves silly using the ruler to show each other the 'measurements' of men of their acquaintance.

It had all been in fun between the two girls, two college girls drinking and being silly in their room late at night but she wondered if she could go back to Maggie now and boast of 'her' specimen.

In any event, she was finally glad to understand the curious mixture of satin-soft and rock-hard an erect cock produced.

If only she knew who her masked man was, and how to ascertain whether he was her True Mate or not. She had never imagined after six years of studying and socializing at college that she would possibly find him on her final evening. She had resigned herself to talking to her father after returning home about how she would know for certain. Before now she simply hadn't been very interested in finding him.

As a young girl, she had been certain her True Mate was Edward. After he had spurned her offer of engagement and a happy marriage, she had refused to talk about mating or anything to do with finding one's True Mate.

Of course after a few days worth of tears, she had assured her seriously dented heart Edward was destined to be her friend, her playmate but *never* her True Mate. She always seemed to find something more interesting than dating after that debacle.

Her parents, thankfully, had let her be, knowing one day she would become interested once more. And that day seemed to have finally arrived.

Here was a man who made her panties damp, who drove her wild with burning lust, and she didn't even know who he was. He kissed like a Greek god, had a rock-hard cock that brought all kinds of wicked ideas into her head, and she simply couldn't decide whether to go with her lusts or try to remain chaste. Never had she been so tempted before.

Thankfully, he finally made the decision for her. Her brain was too stunned and numb to possibly think coherently. He pulled back and she had to clench her hands, digging her stick-on nails into her palms, to stop herself from dragging him back onto her body. She wasn't sure she wanted to come onto him too hard and fast or he might get the wrong idea.

Only the vibrating lust running through him, the obvious reluctance he had for moving, boosted her esteem. He might be retreating but, like her, he didn't seem to want to.

"That was a fantastic appetizer, Sweet One. What other charms do you have to offer a roving pirate?"

Christiana smiled. She was an old hand at sexual banter and flirting.

"Oh, I have plenty of charms, Pirate. I just don't throw them away on the dross. I'm waiting for the gold to arrive."

The dark, warm chuckle emitted from his chest drew her. She *knew* he was familiar but she almost didn't want to figure him out. He was a mystery, one she would hold close to her heart when she returned home. A part of her wanted to know who he was, that he could make her blood race and her heart sing, but a larger part of her always wanted to keep the memories of tonight as a secret, hidden thrill. Something she could ponder over and smile at secretively over her hot chocolate.

The pirate leaned forward, breaking the chill breeze that had struck up. He reached out to twine a golden curl that had fallen out of her French twist around his thick, long finger.

"What if you've already met the gold and cast it aside?"

Christiana frowned. What could he mean? Had he asked her out and had she stupidly turned him down? No! She couldn't have, not this man. His touch was electric, his scent was beguiling and she itched to remove the mask and bandana, to run her hands through his dark curls and outline the ridges of his face. She couldn't possibly have turned such a masculine, sexy man down. She wasn't blind!

"I hope I haven't turned such gold down. But if temporary insanity *had* overtaken me, I sincerely hope I would get a second chance at it."

Realizing she was seriously considering exploring her sexuality with this pirate, Christiana stepped forward, so her body rubbed against his at every possible point.

Christiana felt amazed at the wealth of information her body could pick up with just one long caress. His chest was muscled, yet fiercely warm. It amazed her, the strength and power one could feel from such a simple piece of anatomy.

Her pirate's legs bracketed her, protecting and enticing at the same time. For a moment, she entertained the fantasy of removing his shirt and seeing how much hair sprinkled his chest, and what it felt like to run one's hands through it.

She ached with the desire to touch and feel every inch of his flesh, to explore all his hidden, masculine places and find which areas made him groan and which ones drove him wild with desire.

With snap-decision resolve, Christiana decided to unmask her pirate and find out once and for all who he was. Once she knew him, she felt certain she would be comfortable enough to want to sleep with him, even if it would ruin the mystery and some of the romance.

As her hand reached up to remove his mask, her pirate froze. Thinking he was about to object to her removing his mask, she opened her mouth to reassure him, only to hear her name being called.

"Chrissy! Chrissy, where are you?"

"Chrissy?" the pirate mocked. She nearly snarled in muted frustration.

"That's Maggie, my roommate. She *knows* how much I hate anyone shortening my name. It's designed to get my attention."

"*No one* calls you by a shortened name?" he mocked.

Christiana shrugged, her mind whirling on how to get rid of Maggie without having an in-depth explanation that would last forever if her friend realized her intentions. Her friend meant well, knew full well her position on sex and the men here on campus. But this pirate might be different.

Not really thinking, she answered mechanically.

"An old childhood friend calls me Christi. It's way too far down the track to convince him otherwise. And I sorta like it, not that I'd ever admit it. Everyone else calls me Christiana or finds themselves with a knee in the groin."

The pirate winced, though she didn't notice it. "The friend must be grateful."

"Hmm?"

Reluctantly pulling her body away from the warmth of his, she looked up to her pirate.

"I'll just go tell her not to worry. I'll only be a moment."

In the shadows, she couldn't really see her pirate's eyes, only the gleam from the lights inside the ballroom.

"I'll come back for you later, Sweet One. Go soothe your friend. I think she's getting worried."

Reluctant to leave, Christiana moved forward for one last kiss. Pouring all her passion and frustration into it, she swore as she pulled away.

Running out into the light, she returned to her friend, cursing in a manner that her father and uncles would *still* wash her mouth out with soap for.

Deep in her soul she knew it would be useless to go back into the moonlight and the trees in the extended gardens.

Her pirate would be long gone.

Chapter Four

ೲ

For what felt like the twentieth time that night, Christiana turned over restlessly. Not for the first time, she wished for just once she wasn't so organized and nearly packed to go. Getting up and shoving all her possessions into trunks and boxes would be a huge relief. Instead, she had to lie here quietly, so not to wake Maggie.

Instead, she had to lie in her bed, ultrasensitized. The silky sheets rasped against her heated skin, her clit ached for her mystery pirate's fingers. No matter how much she tried, she couldn't stop her blood thrumming through her veins and the dampness from pooling between her legs.

Fantasy after fantasy of her pirate played through her mind. Of how he would feel lying above her, or below her, or pressed up against the tree and any number of other scenarios. Tossing and turning, desperately trying to cool the heat in her veins, Christiana wished for any task to do to keep her mind occupied.

If she had an excuse—such as packing—Maggie wouldn't complain at the lamp being on, or at rustling noises as Christiana packed and cursed and tried to keep herself busy instead of mooning over some stranger.

Who the hell was the pirate? And why hadn't she noticed how sexy he was before tonight? The final night?

Over and over she had run through her various friends and acquaintances through college and she simply couldn't put a name to him. She *knew* she recognized him. That zinging feeling of familiarity wouldn't go away. Yet, she was stumped when she tried to picture him out of the mask and in a lecture somewhere.

Before bed, she had been going through old yearbooks, trying to remember if he was a guy she'd had a crush on earlier in her college years, who'd already graduated and moved on—but then how would he have entered the ball? It had been strictly monitored by security, the previous few years' balls having been crashed by drunken younger students.

Finally admitting she wouldn't fall asleep, Christiana pulled on a worn pair of jeans and a favorite woolen sweater and crept silently out of the room. The moon was half-full and hopefully a casual stroll around her small garden, soaking up the moon beneath the huge old tree, would calm her down.

For a moment, she wished she were back at home in the forest. A moonlit romp in the woods would clear the cobwebs and desire from her head and body. Even though technically she could change whenever she pleased, more often than not the pull of the moon, the full moon in particular, would compel her to change and run wild.

Over the few years she had spent here in college, she had excused and worked her way around each month's full moon. For the most part, no one cared if a student didn't turn up to one day's worth of classes, as long as assignments were handed in on time. So her day's journey back home, her nightly romp in the woods and the speedy journey back to class went mostly unnoticed.

Christiana mulled over her strange combination of feelings. She resented the restriction of not being able to change at whim or will here at college, resented having to hide a part of herself deeply away, yet the personal freedom here was immense compared to being at home.

Smiling, she listened to her inner demon.

What are they going to do, Christi-girl? Expel you? You've already graduated…might as well go out with a bang! Besides, no one will see you and who the hell cares, even if they do? Let's be wild for once!

Strange how she had never noticed until tonight how much her inner demon sounded and acted like Edward, whispering naughty suggestions in her ear. Taunting her to go further, be more impulsive than she ever let herself be.

Angling herself deeper in the woods, she found her steps lengthen with her purpose. For practically all her life she'd been good. Pranks and childish tantrums aside, she had always done what she felt was right.

And now, on the verge of heading home to fulfill her "destiny", she made another of her snap decisions.

Screw protocol. Stuff her inner voice of caution. She wanted to run in the moonlight, so she bloody well was going to run.

Looking about briefly, she made sure no one had lost their mind and was around. The woods were denser here, nowhere near as lovely as the ones back home, but beggars were never choosers.

Smiling hugely, she stripped her woolen sweater up over her head, her nipples puckering in the chilly breeze. She hadn't bothered with a bra. Who needed one for a moonlit romp anyway?

Dancing around a little from foot to foot, she shed her sneakers and socks and slipped her jeans down over her hips. Bright pink silken panties were carefully folded and placed in the jean pockets. No one liked dirt in their panties. That done, she was ready to go.

For a moment or two, she stood naked and chilly in the dark, dark woods. The moon glowed over her, heating her blood just like the sun did.

Closing her eyes, Christiana silently thanked the woods and the land for the joy and freedom she had experienced over the last few years here at the college.

Then with hardly a thought, she shimmered and Changed.

Chapter Five

ଇ

Edward stood entranced, staring at the naked Christiana in front of him. He had come back hoping she would be restless enough to sit in her garden so he could talk to her. When she had seemed so pensive he had hesitated in interrupting her. Maybe it would be better for her to chew over her own thoughts for a while.

While he procrastinated like an old biddy, she had wandered into the woods. He followed, arguing heatedly within himself.

When she had paused, he too stopped, wondering what was going on in her complex mind. As she had stripped, the air had rushed from his lungs and his knees had wobbled.

When the hell was the last time my knees have wobbled? he thought, incredulous.

The moon shone down over her pale skin, her golden curls framed her face and fell down long enough for a man to enjoy grabbing a handful of them. Her ripe, firm breasts teased and begged for his mouth, his hands, his touch.

When she had shimmered, he felt his cock spring to attention. *Ah man, when was the last time we ran together?*

Feeling like the worst kind of voyeur, Edward hastily stripped out of his Pirate's gear on the other edge of the clearing. Changing, himself, he followed a few paces behind his beautiful wolf-lady. He reveled in her scent, enjoyed loping after her more than he could ever recall or believe. He desperately craved jumping over her, tussling in their wolf form, but more, playing and teasing with her as they always had.

41

Yet he didn't want to tip his hand. If he revealed himself to her now, she would put the pieces together, realize her romantic, mysterious pirate was in fact her old friend, whom she refused to see sexually.

Much as it ached him to admit it, he wanted to keep their fantasy intact.

So for now he stalked her like the animal he was, biding his time, waiting to pounce.

He loved to play Chase and this game was far more exciting. He was chasing fantastic, rock-your-world sex, chasing the woman to whom no one else could measure up.

Chasing Love, a small part of his mind insisted.

As Christiana turned around and loped back to the spot where she had left her clothes, Edward circled back himself. He didn't know whether he was chasing love or not. But he certainly felt as if he were *chasing* Christiana and for now that was more than enough trouble on his plate.

Chapter Six

௸

Christiana pulled her clothes back on more slowly this time. Her mind had settled remarkably well. The run had cleared her mind and soul. Her brain was still full and busy but her emotions were far more under control.

She hadn't lost her independence, hadn't lost the woman she had become, and so everything else could be worked out.

Strangely, she had felt...chased...during her run. Not in a bad sense, not that running-and-never-getting-anywhere-nightmare-style chased. Just...as if someone was chasing her, keeping pace behind her just out of sight.

She didn't feel bad and didn't feel pressured and so she refused to worry about it. No use fighting herself or chasing her tail. If she couldn't see someone chasing her there was no use in worrying over it.

Besides, her instincts were sound. If she didn't feel threatened more than likely nothing was wrong.

Christiana pondered all of her thoughts as she re-tied the laces on her sneakers and began to wander again back to the moonlit gardens. She was heading home the day after tomorrow and, while having unlimited access to the old woods would be a welcome relief, not to mention seeing her parents and family, a part of her would miss the freedom and independence she had found here at college.

Her father's pack was largely spread out now, no longer the old feudal system of her Grandfather's age, yet there were still businesses to take care of and control, huge chunks of wildlife to preserve and other necessary tasks.

Coming to a halt near one of her favorite old trees, she sat down on the damp grass and crossed her legs Indian-style. Slowly, deliberately, Christiana took a deep, calming breath.

Letting it *whoosh* out her lungs, she looked up to the half-full moon. Even half-full, it drew her, pulled at all her senses. More than most women Christiana felt sure she felt more constricted by society than other women. Also her unusually strong sense of morals and devotion to the Pack and its ways often made her feel constricted.

She knew changing out here in the open was, while not a hanging offense or anything, still wrong. Before she could feel even a spark of guilt her musings were interrupted.

"It *is* beautiful, isn't it?" a husky voice intruded on her thoughts.

Whirling around, staining her jeans from the damp grass, she turned to see the pirate leaning against the tree behind her.

"Even only half-full, She draws one. Taunting us lesser creatures with how beautiful and full She *can* be, while keeping the rest of herself hidden from view. Much like you, Sweet One."

Christiana frowned. "What do you mean?"

"I mean the manner you keep those enticing breasts secreted away, hidden from our male gazes, those long, lean legs encased in things like jeans and baggy sweatpants. Do you really think we can't see through them to the slim, elegant legs you sometimes show off? Or hide those luscious breasts, make us not realize how full and round they are and how lovely they'd feel in the palms of our hands?"

Christiana stood up, feeling embarrassed and angry.

"I don't hide, I simply dress to please myself. Jeans are *comfortable*, Pirate. Why should a woman have to dress up all the time simply to become eye candy for a man? This is not the Middle Ages. We women can dress as we please."

The pirate grinned, a huge, delighted grin.

"Temper, temper, Sweet One. I was merely making a comparison between you and the moon. Most women would find that romantic."

Despite herself, Christiana smiled. "I'm not most women."

"I know," he acknowledged. "Most women would not drive me to such desperate straights as dressing up as a pirate."

For the first time since he appeared, Christiana noticed he had removed the bandana, though not the mask. His hair sprung out in all directions, black as the night and curly in a cute, but still masculine way. She noticed he wore a thick gold loop in one ear, a very piratical earring.

"Did you pierce your ear for the ball?" she queried, the earring tugging on her memory for some reason. There was some significance here but her muddled brain couldn't bring it out. That earring meant something, reminded her of something…

"No, and for a wench, you ask far too many questions."

Coming forward, he pulled her into his arms. Against her will, her hands rose up to run gently through his curls. They were soft to the touch, obviously well-cared for. As she tugged his curls, he bent his head and kissed her.

Christiana found herself holding her breath, hoping the electric feelings she felt last time were some sort of hormonal fluke. But they weren't. A river of desire flooded her, drenching her pussy, making her nipples stand out and rub against her woolen sweater. She arched her back and moaned, lost in the flood of desire and ache to be possessed. She was losing her mind!

Tightening her hands, she felt the strong, silky curls twine with her fingers. She dimly noticed his hands were running under her sweater, touching her skin lightly. He had a feather touch.

She could feel his rough fingers tracing lines up and down her back but it was so gentle, so soft, she barely felt it.

He groaned and deepened the kiss, she opened her mouth to allow him in.

"Why aren't you wearing a bra?" he murmured against her mouth as he licked her lips.

Christiana smiled.

"I wasn't expecting to meet up with a pirate in my backyard. I don't sleep in a bra and I simply pulled on jeans and a sweater."

She smiled around their kiss as he bent her back further into the tree, arching her into his embrace.

"There should be a law," he husked, palming her breasts and rubbing her straining nipples. "You must wear a bra at all times, except in bed. These luscious breasts would tempt a saint."

"But you're a pirate," she laughed, "not a saint."

"I know."

With that, he pulled up her sweater, bunching it around her neck. He bent down and took a mouthful of breast. His wicked tongue licked her nipple, his mouth creating a warm, wet, sucking vacuum.

The electrical pleasure, the indescribable joy he made her feel, had her arching further in to him and crying out with the new and unexplored sensations. She had played with her own nipples, had even read of mammary orgasms, but never, *never* had she felt such pleasure radiating from her nipples.

Suddenly, she found her lips covered with her pirate's, his hands were back to tweaking her nipples, playing with her breasts.

His mouth covering hers, he muttered, "Scream for me, Sweet One."

When he did something with his fingers, creating an electric shaft of pleasure bolting through her, she cried out again and he swallowed her cry.

"Just like honey, sweet and seductive enough to snare a man forever."

"What?" she breathed, her mind screaming at her in recognition and alarm. If only she could breathe for a second and *think*.

"Don't think," he said, as if replying to her internal monologue, "just feel *this*."

Deftly, he unsnapped her jeans and slid a warm, strong hand inside her panties.

"Ahh," he murmured against her cheek, "so you *do* sleep in panties. For the last five minutes I'd been wondering."

Christiana knew she had made a sound but it was from deep inside her chest and sounded quite wild. Her pirate was stroking her, petting her *right* on her clit and driving her wild. Even through the silk of her panties she knew his fingers were getting damp. She was creaming, flowing like a river, and he was simply making her cream more.

He stroked and stroked, as if she was a cat or animal to be petted.

Christiana knew her body well enough to know very soon she would reach her climax and scream. Wanting to take him with her, she grabbed his pants, pulling him closer to her.

"Uh-uh, Sweet One, this one is for you."

"But..."

Muddled with lust and unusual amounts of desire running through her system, she didn't give much resistance to her Pirate. She let him grab both of her wrists, chaining them tightly together in one of his hands.

Christiana smiled, tried not to laugh. Here she was "going with the flow" as Maggie and a number of her girl-friends had urged her to do time and time again and her Pirate was getting all dominant on her.

Strange how she had been the dominant person in most of her relationships since she was a young teenager. Yet here she was, happily letting a man mould her to his wishes, and all it was doing to her was making her horny as hell.

She didn't feel the least amount of panic or an urge to scream and run or bash his head in. She found it sexy and disturbingly *right*. She must need to get laid more than she had ever realized.

With one hand chaining both her much smaller ones together, her sexy pirate could no longer tweak her nipple. Christiana momentarily mourned the loss but her pirate more than made up for it by slowly, warmly, sexily replacing his hand back down her damp panties.

With a grin and an evil twinkle in his eye, he watched her flush and pant for breath, enjoyed every second of her and her body's reaction to him as he continued to stroke her clit. As aroused as she was with their intimate play and sexual acts, her Pirate drew in a sharp breath and bent his head down to once more suck her breast.

Christiana writhed, wanting more of his caress, yet also wanting to pull away from the swamping pleasure. This somehow felt different from how she pleasured herself.

When she played with herself, learned how to use the toys and paraphernalia she had collected over her time here in college, she felt arousal, yes, but not to this degree. Not this drugging, mind-numbingly intense arousal.

The intensity of her reaction to this pirate scared her on some gut level. It felt almost as if he were made for her.

Christiana immediately shut the door on those sorts of thoughts and went back to analyzing her own reactions. She was panting, straining against him. It was a frustrating mockery of the sexual act, yet it was perfect at the same time.

The moon shone down on them both, bathing them in Her blessing, heating the wolf's blood in her veins and making her want to nip at her pirate, claim him as her own.

Claim him? her brain echoed in stunned shock. *She didn't even know who he was!*

As if in response, the moon came out from behind a thin cloud and the whole backyard was lit as bright as day for her. She turned her head to catch the profile of her almost-lover and gasped.

Her pirate continued sucking her breast and stroking her, assuming her gasp had been yet another sexual response, but Christiana was trying to marshal a few half-coherent thoughts together.

It couldn't possibly be...?

Before she could even finish the thought that had entered her brain, she felt her whole body seize up. The reaction was familiar to her, yet the intensity of the orgasm crashing through her was not.

Her pussy clenched, her nipples tightening even more, Christiana threw her head back, not even knowing what her body was doing to her, and opened her mouth to scream her release at the moon.

Her body shuddered over and over again, her Pirate still gently stroking her through the orgasm. She felt the flood of moisture leaking out her body and covering her Pirate's fingers and soaking her panties even more. In her own strange way, her brain registered that, as much as he had branded her, she had also branded him.

As she came down from her high, she shuddered at the sensitive way her body still picked up his fingers stroking her. Trying to wrestle her arms free, she struggled.

"Stop. Don't...too sensitive," she panted.

"Now, now, I'm a pirate, remember? I think we can pull one more orgasm from you before I head off to my ship. Just once more, Sweet One," he coaxed her, the loss of his lips feeling incredibly cold in the night air, daring her with the twinkle in his eye to push herself further.

Christiana tried to squirm, to work out if his continued strokes were pleasurable or painful. Her sensitive skin and clit were throbbing heatedly, so she felt extra-sensitive to his strokes.

Christiana had tried a few times to push herself to a second release quickly on the heels of her first but the explosive release after her orgasms always made her so weak and tired, she could never keep up the pace necessary to push herself into another.

Yet, here was her pirate, gently pushing her further than she could take herself, giving her something she had tried for a few times, but never been able to reach.

She gasped, she panted, she writhed and, after a few minutes, completely taken by surprise, she came again, screaming even louder this time, uncaring if she woke the entire college dormitory, as her second orgasm ripped through her.

Weak and spent, she muttered her thanks as her pirate lowered her onto the soft, grassy ground, flinching slightly at the loss of his fingers inside her. He sat beside her, cradling her in his arms.

He gently kissed her cheek, soothing her as she caught her breath.

"Next time," he promised, "I'll take you further."

"I don't think I'll survive that," she chuckled. "Anyway, I'm going home the day after tomorrow...mmpf."

Christiana found her lips pressed together by his fingers, silencing her words for the first time since she had been a kid.

"Let's not speak of that just now. I have to go and you should get to bed."

He kissed her lingeringly and she wallowed in the exquisite taste of his mouth. It was a taste she would never forget.

All too soon for her newly emerged emotions, her Pirate pulled himself away from her lips, dragged his hands away from her body. Surprised, Christiana felt the chill night wind whipping around the trees and gardens. She noted how, strangely, in her Pirate's arms she hadn't felt anything except the burning heat of both their bodies.

Rubbing her arms, pulling her sweater back down, she clenched her mouth shut tightly as her Pirate pulled himself away. He wasn't harsh or rude about it, yet he firmly, purposefully untangled them from one another.

Christiana refused to say a thing. She wasn't some weak, stupid heroine from a cheesy romance novel. She wouldn't whimper or beg or plead. He didn't owe her anything and she wouldn't make a fool of herself.

With barely a word—he was a pirate after all—her romantic masked man stood up and headed off, deep into the night.

Christiana watched and tried to reconcile the image of her childhood friend and teenage crush with the huge, masked man she had just double-orgasmed with. Something was up and she had no idea how to play along with his game without unmasking him.

Yawning, she headed back inside, stripped and climbed into bed. The silky feel of her sheets made her smile but, as she lay down and tried to work out what she was going to do, she drifted off before even a half-decent plan could form.

There was always tomorrow morning.

Chapter Seven

ॐ

Christiana opened her eyes to stare at the crystal wind chimes making multicolored patterns on her ceiling.

What to do?

For well over five years now Edward had been trying to convince her to have an affair with him. Ever since she had headed off to college.

He had tried any number of arguments and persuasions, none of them changing her mind. She had offered her fourteen-year-old heart to him on a platter and he had rejected it.

He had been well over seventeen, and about to head out into the big wide world. College and then wherever his feet took him, she believed had been his words.

Even so, she had felt at nearly fourteen she was old enough to know her own mind.

More fool she.

While she still loved him—how could you *not* love a man on whom you'd had a crush for long as you could recall?—she had never again let him know how much he affected her.

So why was he dressing up as a pirate and seducing the hell out of her? Revenge? Just to get into her pants?

Even more importantly, should she unmask him? Let him know she knew it was him? Or should she play along? If she played along *knowing* it was Edward, when he unmasked himself, expecting her to be shocked and surprised, wouldn't it be lovely to calmly stare at him and say she had guessed back on the very first night?

Appealing as that idea was she squirmed to think of all the ground she would lose if she traveled this way. She had spent *years* convincing him she didn't want him, that she wasn't attracted to him. If she followed his tune, *knowing* who he was, he would never again believe she didn't care for him.

It was a messy coil.

Next to her, she heard Maggie yawn and grumble as her clock radio went off. Smiling, knowing the routine extremely well, Christiana huddled safely under her bedclothes. After sharing a room with the girl for almost the entire six years they had shared together at college, Christiana knew when to duck for cover.

For perhaps the last time, Maggie, still mostly asleep, unplugged the cheap-ass clock radio from the bedside table between their twin beds and hurled it across the floor of their tiny room. Not only did the music stop but an incredibly familiar *crunch* sound emanated from the poor battered machine.

Christiana giggled. That one had almost lasted the entire week. It appeared to be a stronger model than most. She made a mental note to get the same brand this time.

Well-versed in the different noises a clock radio makes when thrown against a wall, Christiana decided they would now be buying their ninetieth clock radio from the cheap Wal-Mart in town. The check-out clerks knew them well.

"Come on Maggs, time to wake up," she laughed, sitting up and stretching. Once, back in their first year, Maggie had accidentally thrown the clock across the room, knocking her on the head.

Since then, Christiana had been sure to either not be in the room when the alarm went off, or to be safely hidden beneath the covers. Maggie had a wicked throw.

Climbing out of bed, she went over to the bureau and picked out clean underwear, a sloppy T-shirt and pair of sweatpants. They needed to clean the dorm this morning from top to bottom, and then start hauling their stuff out to their cars.

Christiana was hoping the day of cleaning and talking to Maggie would help her sort out in her mind what to do with her pirate.

Dragging the coverlet from Maggie, she was startled when the *whomph* of her pillow caught her right across the head.

"What the…?"

Next thing she knew, Maggie had pulled herself up on her knees and was thrashing her with the pillow.

Laughing, Christiana reached over to her own bed and grabbed her own pillow.

"I'm so going to get you for winning that last pillow fight. You were unfair! Pinning me by using your chocolates as a peace offering was a foul trick!"

Christiana laughed. Back in their first year they had fought over who got to use which beds, finally ending up in a huge, shrieking pillow fight. Christiana had indeed offered Maggie her box of Godiva milk chocolates to settle the fight, and then pinned Maggie until she yielded.

It had been dirty, but worth getting the bed underneath the window.

Laughing, Christiana tried to wrestle and fight Maggie but her friend was determined.

Eventually, she yielded.

* * * * *

"Aaahhh, so the lamented Edward strikes again. Why didn't you say so? I wouldn't have interfered. I know you've been saving your cherry for him. It's about damn time one of you wises up and you fuck each other."

Christiana rolled her eyes and scrubbed the floor harder, with larger, more vicious strokes.

"You don't understand, Maggie."

Her roommate laughed. "I'm not stupid, hon, of course I understand. You've had the hots for each other since you were little rugrats but you never got it on at the same time. As kids, you wanted him, as young adults he wanted you. Now you're both trying to move on and neither of you can because there's still this massive unresolved sexual tension between you."

Christiana muttered curses under her breath. It had taken her *months* of self-reflection upon first arriving at college to work that out and, even then, it hadn't helped solve any of her problems. How dare Maggie understand so easily!

Stealing a glance over her shoulder, she saw her best friend sitting on her knees, scrubbing brush in hand and huge grin on her face.

"What?" she grumbled.

"It took you ages to work out that's what the electric attraction was, didn't it?"

Refusing to give her the pleasure of answering, Christiana continued to scrub. "So, almighty all-knowing beast of a friend. What do I do? Do I unmask him, or carry on with the fantasy?"

"Hmm," Maggie contemplated. Christiana could practically hear her thinking, turning over different possibilities.

"Scrub while you think or we'll never get the candle wax off this damn floor. Are you sure this happened at our last Halloween bash? I could swear they were here when we arrived!"

"I'm sure," Maggie stated. "You were far too plastered to remember. I, on the other hand, was fuming over Ian being late, so I hadn't started drinking when you spilled the wine or started boasting of that stunt with the wax. But that's beside the point. I'm trying to think what I'd do in your situation. You want passion and romance, right?"

"Right."

"But you don't want to go all the way with this Edward."

For the briefest of seconds, Christiana had a mental flash so real, so life-like she was grateful to already be sitting on the floor. Otherwise she might have melted and created more of a mess to clean up.

Heated bodies, straining toward each other, slick with sweat as moans filled the air. Edward's large, warm, rough hands caressing her skin, causing an electric current that made her knees weak. His thick, hot erection paused at her entrance. The strength of his body and mind preparing her for his possession; body and soul. Before her vision could become any more mouth-watering, she firmly squashed it. She had a floor to scrub.

Remembering to answer her friend, she paused in her furious scrubbing and agreed absently.

"Right."

"Okay, so I'd probably unmask him and then make a deal with him."

Christiana frowned and stopped scrubbing. "Huh?"

"Well," Maggie explained, "you want the passion and romance, but none of the penetrating sex. There are, as I *know* you've found out, a heap of things you can do *without* actual intercourse. There's no point stringing each other along, Edward would have to unveil himself soon—like before you go home tomorrow. He can't just *appear* in costume and mask at your parent's home and expect you to not work out who he is. So take control of the situation. Unmask him when he undoubtedly turns up tonight, and then offer him a deal."

Christiana sat back and thought of it. She imagined an "anything goes but penetration" deal between her and Edward, and then thought of all the things he could do to her—and even better, all the things she could tease him with.

Flushing, she looked back to Maggie.

"You're not just a pretty face, are you? Anyone would think you had a Bachelor's degree in Business Management and Communications."

Maggie beamed. "Does this mean you'll finish the wretched floor?"

Christiana looked scornful. "Don't be stupid. Get back to scrubbing."

Chapter Eight

ଚଠ

Christiana fidgeted with the hem of her micro miniskirt. Having never worn the blasted thing she hadn't realized *just* how short it was. She had bought it as a fashion impulse back in her sophomore year, and then never quite had the guts and right situation appear at the same time.

A very pretty navy blue, it complemented her eyes, while the midriff-baring white shirt showed off her faint tan and blonde curls.

She knew she looked good, she just wasn't sure it would do any good. Looking good in the past had never seemed to affect Edward yet this time *he* had started the game. Maybe things would be different for a change.

Unable to remain still, she began to pace back and forth before the large tree in her dorm backyard.

She wasn't *worried*-worried, she was simply *nervous*-worried, she consoled herself. Who wouldn't be nervous? Seducing Edward had been a long-held fantasy of hers. She had mostly given up on it years ago—just before she left for college, in fact—but she was disgusted to realize that, with a simple action of dressing up and masking himself, he had seduced her more thoroughly than any man had in five years of college.

A deeply hidden part of her acknowledged she had fallen hard and fast for her childhood friend, *again!*

Of course, the rest of her disputed the fact vehemently. Never again would she fall for the man who, as a child, she had been certain was hers and hers alone. He had been with many women over the years, probably *hundreds* since she had given up and stopped trailing after him like a nuisance.

Neither was she interested in being some trophy or plaything for a man. Her True Mate would accept her power and position in the Pack as its eventual leader, and love her simply as she was. She would give him her faithfulness, her loyalty and the satisfaction of truly knowing she only belonged to him.

Yet in the meantime, she wouldn't mind playing a bit with good old Edward. A bit of experience never hurt a girl and with a no-penetration clause on their playtime...

Before her thoughts could circle back and she could start worrying all over again, she heard muffled footfalls behind her. If she hadn't been listening so keenly for it, she would never have heard him.

Christiana berated herself. She should have realized his uncanny quietness should have been an indicator to his true identity. No real *human* could walk that quietly and sneak up on *her*.

She watched him come closer, still dressed as her pirate, still masked, but his curls once again left free and wild. His hair had grown since she had seen him at Christmas, yet she should never have forgotten those wild curls. She squashed the feeling of being incredibly stupid.

Might as well dive right in and go for the balls of the matter.

Before he could even open his mouth in greeting or draw her to him, she spoke right up.

"Hey there, Edward. Been a while, hasn't it? What's new?"

More than twenty years of studying the man came in good stead. She noticed the very slight tremor along his jaw as a muscle flexed. She also noticed the very faint hitch in his step. However, to practically anyone else, he would not have seemed to falter in the slightest.

"Not a lot, Christi-girl. It's only been since Christmas so I thought I'd spice up your Graduation Ball. You were rather insistent on the desire for romance and passion. I thought I did rather well."

"Oh, you did fantastically well. It was the merest fluke I recognized you late last night. You do make a brilliant pirate."

He bowed, an elegant, courtly gesture that had her heart fluttering madly.

Frowning, Christiana tried to hide her reaction. It took her a moment to realize he was practically on top of her when he straightened up.

He held her arm and pulled her closer before she could even reorient herself.

Leaning forward, he kissed her, hard. This was no courtly peck. This was the pirate, plundering and taking all he could get. Moaning, Christiana opened her mouth and let him in. She couldn't fight herself and him. She might as well let him win the small battles and save herself for the war.

Or that's what she convinced herself, anyway.

Breathing deeply, he finally pulled himself away. "Now *that* was more the sort of welcome I was expecting."

Christiana smiled a little sadly. "Well, you still got it. Let's walk and we can work this out."

Determined not to seem at a disadvantage by pacing, Christiana set out at a brisk walk across the gardens and into the much larger college grounds. Edward kept pace with her easily, as he always had.

"What's there to work out, Christi-girl? We're going to have a grand old time together, thoroughly get each other out of our systems and move on."

She shook her head, unable to believe the stupidity of men.

"That never works, even *you* have to realize that. And I certainly am not going to change my beliefs and morals just for you. We're going to set ground rules and stick to them."

Even behind the mask, Christiana could see Edward raising an eyebrow at her in that mocking way he had.

"Oh really. You don't think I could seduce you?"

"I don't think you could get into my pants, no. Many guys here have tried and I've managed to resist them all. I doubt you're any better."

She rushed on before he could contradict her.

"Besides, my rules are what count here. If you want to play so badly, I don't think you'll feel very cheated. My only rule is no penetration."

Edward came to a halt, forcing her to stop as well. He looked her over very, very carefully.

"That's your *only* rule," he repeated slowly, "no penetration?"

Christiana rolled her eyes.

"I'm not an idiot. Just like every other horny girl alive I've had cravings and desires. There is such a thing as masturbation and other assorted *methods* of relief. I'm not some ignorant virgin. I'm merely saving my virginity for someone who will truly appreciate it," she hurried on, *knowing* what he was about to say in that way both of them had. "I mean my True Mate. Some hormonal man who has had the hots for me for a while, no offense to you, simply doesn't count in my book anymore."

She felt the weight of his stare for a minute, and then it dragged out to two. She resisted the impulse to babble in the silence.

"No penetration," he finally spoke.

Christiana nodded. "No penetration," she confirmed, all her stubbornness and belief behind her long-ago decision holding firm and showing in her simple statement.

"Anything else goes?"

Christiana thought. She didn't mind experimenting. She was, in fact, wet with anticipation. She simply wanted to keep her hymen intact and make sure the first and only cock to ever enter her was her destined mate. A "no penetration" rule amply covered that.

She nodded again, more slowly.

"As long as you don't count this as a technicality. You know what I mean—what the spirit of my deal is. I want to stay chaste, just not necessarily pure. But as long as you're following the spirit of my deal, anything else goes."

Edward grinned at her, a feral, wild grin she had never seen from him. It was lustful and truly wild. She swallowed, suddenly wondering why he was so desperate to seduce her. It wasn't like he didn't have a million other women throwing themselves all over him.

Before she could think, or even attempt to articulate the questions buzzing around her mind, he stuck out his hand.

"We have a deal, Christi-girl."

Chapter Nine

෨

Edward felt triumph unlike anything else when Christiana placed her smaller hand in his and began to shake it. The trap was set; the bait had been taken. Now all he needed was patience and luck, just like any other hunter.

When Christiana had unmasked him, he had known his plans weren't crumbling, merely being brought to a head faster than expected. He had fully expected to unmask himself to her tonight, after attempting to seduce her.

His masking had, in fact, lasted longer than he had hoped. He *knew* deep in his soul that he would have recognized Christiana in any mask, any costume, anywhere in the world. Her eyes, her curls and her beautiful, rounded body called to him on some instinctive level that he finally had given up fighting.

He didn't want to delve into his subconscious and discover if they really were True Mates. While the thought itself held some appeal, the reality of finding himself tied for eternity to not only his childhood playmate, but also the future leader of the Pack, was incredibly daunting.

He didn't believe himself to be some egotistical man but his ego was certainly masculine enough that, in front of the Pack, *always* having to let Christiana have the last word and power rankled a bit.

He knew her well enough to know she'd never lord it over him, in any sense. He had found himself surprised four years ago to not know her well enough if she was the sort of woman who would let *him* be dominant in the bedroom, or if her power needed to extend into her whole life.

They were damn close and the oldest of buddies. For a fling, for an affair, that was more than enough for him for now. The point was, he would have known her in any disguise and it had been a minor blow to his ego to realize *she* didn't instantly recognize *him*.

The fact that some minor gesture had given him away gave him hope. If she knew his body language, knew his gestures and impulses, then there was some hope left for his battered ego—no matter how fun it had been to seduce her and prove her instinctual reaction to him was there.

On a totally different level, her "no penetration" clause was even *more* enthralling. What better seduction tactic for either of them to know there was a point to which they both must stop? Christiana would feel safe, knowing that they could do anything except technically have sex, and he could try to rise to the challenge.

According to *her* rule of no penetration, he would play the gentleman and adhere to it. Yet he knew himself, and her, well enough to know that eventually their passionate play would come to a peak. He snickered at the thought.

Having Christiana beg him to fuck her senseless was a particularly pleasant fantasy he had been indulging in for more months than he cared to admit. And if she *did* plead such to him, he would be more than happy to make her eat her "no penetration" clause, and give them both the satisfaction they craved.

He tried to suppress his chuckle. Oh yeah, he couldn't have planned it better himself. The added bonus of having Christiana feel as if she were in control was just gravy. She was always that much more mischievous and daring when she felt in control of a situation, had been like that since she was two or three years old and determined to rule the world.

"What are you grinning at?"

Edward paused, realizing he had been grinning like a maniac the last few minutes over his devilish thoughts.

Christiana, obviously seeing his joy and interest in her challenge, had halted a few paces behind.

"Just thinking, Christi-girl. So where is the one place on this campus you've fantasized about seducing some poor unsuspecting man?"

For a long moment, she simply stared at him. Edward worried she was about to back down, call off their deal. She cocked her head in the same manner when thinking as she had since she was a child. Edward relaxed. She was just mulling over everything, scheming in her own manner.

He smiled. He welcomed her pitting her will against his own. They had both been butting heads for years. Being both stubborn and pigheaded had its down sides. It meant they often became too involved in their games of chess and competitions. Why not carry it over into their sexual games? It added life and fun and that little something that was uniquely theirs.

Instead of answering, Christiana took his hand and began to lead him off into a shadowy section of the gardens where large trees had been planted. Edward rolled his eyes, certain she couldn't see him. Trust his Christi not to answer him, but *show* him!

Playing along for the moment—his turn to take the lead would come soon enough—he let her lead him into the lightly wooded section of the grounds. It was nothing compared to their grounds at home but, in a pinch, it would do. The air was scented with pine and fir, smells that reminded him of his home. Like a flash of light, he realized this was Christiana's special place—special in more than just a sexual fantasy place. It was where she came when she felt homesick.

In that instant, Edward made a resolution. No matter how out-of-control everything became, he would make this fantasy of hers special and memorable. If she wanted to be in control, he gritted his teeth in suppressed desire, then he would let her stay in control.

Elizabeth Lapthorne

Even if it killed him.

Chapter Ten

ॐ

Christiana looked around the parkland. She would never admit it but this area had helped save her sanity on more than one occasion. In those first few months, when she was more homesick than she cared to remember, when the ache of not being near her forest, her parents and large family burned like a hole in her chest, she had come here.

It was nothing compared to her forest at home — but then nowhere could replace *her* forest in her heart. Sure, she might be the great-big leader of the Pack one day but, just like her mom was strong enough to stand by her father and help him, so too had she always desired a friend and True Mate strong enough to let her lead.

A part of her mind had always known Naomi had been more than just a fuck-buddy, or even a True Mate, for her Grandfather. She had been his Helpmate, his Companion, his strength when he had needed it.

Men didn't seem to understand that being the voice of power, the leader, wasn't just about leading. Their support network, their friends and family and, most importantly of all, their Mate was just as important as anything else.

Without that special, personal bond from a helpmate, a leader was nothing more than the strongest person, the biggest bully, in the group.

Christiana smiled. It was one of the many, many realizations she had found here in the woods at college.

The soft grass underfoot grounded her, the scent of pine filled her nostrils and, if she closed her eyes and concentrated *really* hard, she could imagine she was home and meditating in her own backyard.

From the silent, reverent way Edward followed her and didn't make teasing comments, she guessed he had worked out how special this place was to her.

Funny how she had driven away all fantasies of them both together here—yet now, here they were. When she had decided to take the offer at this college, she had decided to finally pack away all the childish fantasies of her and Edward.

She knew they couldn't possibly be True Mates—the hurt, the pain he had caused her when he had spurned her offer just before *he* went to college was the start of her knowledge. Since then, she had tried and tried to get him out of her head.

After finally graduating high school, she had decided to get him out of her head and heart. That was a large part of her wanting to get away during college, so she could grow up apart from him and become her own person.

It had been difficult but she had finally convinced herself the connection and bond she felt with Edward was merely from the familiarity of him being the oldest friend she had.

Yet, she always seemed to come back to him, always her thoughts returned to him, it was always him her body craved. She knew full well that trying to satisfy their sexual cravings wouldn't help them in the long run—it would be far better for them to never have sex—yet neither could she simply walk away from him, particularly when he was dressed so appealingly as a pirate.

Her head knew it was foolishness to be sexual with him— even with a 'no penetration' clause—yet her stupid, naïve heart simply wouldn't listen. She had always wanted to explore sexual acts with Edward and here was her chance. Hopefully, she could keep herself busy enough with her new life and responsibilities with the Pack and her work that she wouldn't have to run into him more than absolutely necessary.

Moving on with her life and work was the best thing she could do afterwards.

And so, she led him to her special secluded spot, the place where she meditated and cleared her mind, the place she always began her run when she couldn't get home to change or when she simply couldn't hold back any longer.

It would be a welcome relief next full moon to be able to truly let go and lose herself in her wolf form. Those few, scattered, rare times she had had to change here, she had needed to stay so aware of her surroundings during the whole evening. The amount of energy and willpower she had to expend on keeping her wolf-mind sentient had been incredibly taxing and more than enough reason to do her damndest to make it home each full moon.

The luxury of really being able to let go next full moon, of being home for good, was something she looked forward to more than she could express.

Finally, she stopped at a particularly grassy spot underneath a truly huge tree. "Lie down here," she stated, trying not to sound too impatient.

As always, Edward merely raised an eyebrow, mocking and questioning her judgment. Some things never changed. "Shouldn't you strip? Or me?"

Christiana crossed her arms over her chest, determined to take control of the situation. Edward's turn would evidently come soon enough but, for now, it was her place, her fantasy and, most importantly of all, her rules.

Not even deigning to answer him, she began to tap her foot impatiently.

Edward grinned at her, mocking her silently with his overacting as he lowered himself to the grassy ground. "You never did have any patience, Christi-girl, and I bet you haven't learned how to control that stubborn streak in you, either. Have you?"

Christiana smiled, showing her teeth. She slowly knelt beside him and removed his silk mask, enjoying the revealing of her masked man. Without even answering—she was enjoying this far too much to think at the moment—she began to pull off his black silk pirate shirt.

Finally, she spoke. "You better hope I learned patience, otherwise tonight will be far more fun for me than you. And anyway, who says stubbornness is bad? I rather like it in myself."

Edward began to help her get his shirt off, so she tapped his hands gently.

"My rules."

With a dramatic sigh he complied and let her do the work. When she began to unbuckle his pants without even touching his chest, a muscle in his jaw flexed. Apparently he was getting the idea.

Nothing Edward ever did could be considered passive but the fact that he lay there, with his shirt cast down beside him and his belt being pulled from the loops of his breeches, was about as passive as Christiana had ever seen him.

As she pulled his pants down to his knees, she tried to calm her heart. Sure, she'd seen heaps of porn pictures, and felt her life-like jelly vibrator, but she had never *actually* held a naked, erect penis before.

Penis? Her mind echoed. Despite herself, she sucked in a deep breath as his *cock* surged upwards, saluting her and her femininity.

Pulling his pants down to his knees, she ignored everything but removing the teasing g-string cupping his balls and half-covering his cock.

"Did you wear this last night?" she huskily murmured, her voice having gone all strange on her. She was so excited and enticed she could barely form the words, let alone think coherently.

"What?" he muttered, obviously trying to keep a hold of his lusts. "The thong? Sure. Couldn't really get away with boxers underneath practically see-through pants. Why?"

His flip question made her blood thrum louder. The thought that this itsy scrap of material had been the only thing cupping his immense cock last night was enough to make her feel faint. All this warm, silky skin and flesh had been so close to her. In that instant, she truly understood what men saw in skimpy, see-through lace bra and panty sets.

The thought that a tiny scrap of silk, barely big enough to cover his flaccid cock and balls, was nowhere near enough material to even half-cover his hugely erect cock, made her throat dry out and her heartbeat accelerate.

Reverently, she pulled the tiny male thong down his legs to tangle in the breeches.

With no preliminaries, she bent down to run her tongue along the warm, prickly skin. She was surprised to see the veins bulging. Her life-like vibrator had ridges but she thought they were there for show. She hadn't really thought about how veins carrying all the blood for this fantastic erection would show under the skin of one's cock.

It was so interesting she wished for a moment she had studied anatomy.

As she ran her tongue over and over the warm, smooth skin and traced the lumpy-but-still-soft veins, she was so immersed in her own discovery, she barely registered Edward drawing a deep, shuddering breath.

When this finally penetrated her lust-clogged mind, she noticed him clenching his fists beside his hips. She had read about this in her erotica books and sex manuals. Wasn't there something about men using their hands to direct women's heads when they were getting close to coming?

Shrugging away her questions, she continued exploring this amazing object that had so many names. Love lance, sword, shaft, penis, cock...the list went on and on in her mind as she traced the warm, silky skin.

It was so soft she felt immense curiosity and surprise.

Men didn't moisturize down here, so how does the skin stay so soft and delicate? Must be one of those life's ironies, like women who had them, not being overly fond of large breasts. Yet men across the board and world were entranced by them.

But finally, Christiana understood the term "manhood". Here was an object beautiful and wild, yet so essentially male, women from every walk and station in life were ensnared by it.

"Manhood" might be an old-fashioned term, and practically obsolete in everything except some literature, but it truly captured the manliness ans sexiness of an erect cock to her.

She was surprised by her reaction. Christiana decided she could quite easily and happily spend hours tonguing this enticing piece of flesh, this *manhood,* and still have questions and be curious.

The texture of his cock is strange, she thought. It was just like she had read about in her romance books, in her sex manuals—numerous places. His cock was hard but the skin surrounding it was soft. The fine hairs around his balls made a prickly, delicate sensation, scratchy but not abrasive. It was strange and exciting and all new to her.

Enjoying her discovery of his cock, she opened her mouth fully to enclose the red head of it. She was surprised to feel its heat, the blood really *did* make it hot.

Subconsciously she also heard him moan and smiled as he thrust his hips carefully toward her. Enjoying his reaction, knowing deep in her soul she was bringing him pleasure, she started getting excited and bolder with her explorations. She twirled her tongue around the soft head of his cock.

So many different textures! Her fingers played with the soft skin around the length of his cock, and with the lightly furred balls, feeling the weight of his testicles rolling inside their sac. On top of all that, the very tip of his cock peeked out, letting her tongue taste the interesting saltiness, run around the smooth tip of his cock. It was fascinating and so erotic she had to remind herself to breathe.

After exploring the tip of him, she began running her tongue down his impressive length. As she began to get into a rhythm, she moved her head further and further down his shaft. She relaxed her throat muscles and sucked on him, like she would a lollipop.

Edward groaned even louder and grabbed the back of her head firmly. She smiled around the huge mouthful she held. She had never truly considered what it would be like to drive Edward mad with pleasure.

Oh, she had thought about the many varied ways she could pleasure him, how she would love to try a million different fantasies out with him, yet she had never thought past *what* she would do to him. She had never really thought through *how* he would react.

In some ways she was glad she had never thought so far ahead. His uninhibited response was spurring her on as well as turning her on.

She resisted the impulse to touch herself.

Sucking harder on his cock, she bobbed her head and quickened the pace. Edward tightened his hands in her hair. Christiana closed her eyes and breathed deeply.

The unique yet never forgotten scent of Edward filled her, along with the familiar scent of the forest and trees. Christiana found herself shuddering. It was hard to tell whether this was yet another of her fantasies or if she was finally living her dream of sucking Edward off.

Even with her eyes shut she couldn't be fantasizing the groans coming from Edward's mouth, or the heated thrusts of his thick cock down her throat. It was too intense, too exciting to be a mere fantasy. This was the real thing.

Deciding she had wallowed in her discoveries enough, she decided it was time to show Edward that for a *virgin* she was well read as well as fairly proficient. She sucked hard on the length of his cock, using her tongue to tickle the underside of his head, then started bobbing her head up and down, relaxing her muscles to let the stem go as far back as she could.

As she grew more used to the feelings, both her own sexual responses and the feeling of the first-ever long, hard, *real* cock sliding inside her mouth, she pumped faster and faster. She fisted the few inches she simply couldn't fit down her throat, hoping to give Edward not only the time of his life, but also such an intense blowjob it would literally blow his mind.

It almost surprised her how easy it was. Within a minute of her working him furiously, he moaned and fisted her curls and pulled her even further down his shaft.

"Christi...I'm...oh! *Hell* that's good!"

With that cry, she felt his cock tremble in her mouth. It was the strangest feeling, almost as if he had a separate mind. She could almost feel his shaft quiver and ready itself, and then begin to spurt his seed down her throat. For a moment of madness, she felt as if his cock had a life of its own, as if it were sentient. Then her mouth was flooded with the taste of his salty seed and she was swallowing his essence deep inside her.

The musky, universal scent of sex was in the air between them, the tang that only release can bring. She continued sucking his quickly-deflating cock for a few seconds, determined to wring every last drop of cum from him. As his cock became flaccid, she sat up, licking her lips and tasting his essence on herself.

It was a strange taste, but certainly not a bad one. She grinned. For her first blowjob, she thought she'd done rather well.

She looked at her prone Edward. She felt incredibly happy. An intense, incredibly feminine pride welled deep inside her chest. She felt happy and light and like a million dollars.

"That was a fantastic appetizer," she stated clearly, despite all the giddy sensations building inside herself. "What's for the main course?"

Chapter Eleven

ဢ

Edward looked at the woman he had grown up with. In the blink of an eye he saw a dozen snapshots of them growing up. Her first change, with the joy and self-discovery that had brought her. Her first hunt, where he had followed her to make sure she was safe.

Her first game of field hockey, where she had been tripped up by an opponent and cut her knee. He had rushed to her side, in the middle of the playing field, to hold her and soothe her tears. When he had offered to carry her from the field she had scorned him, retribution shining clearly in her ten-year-old eyes.

The girl who had knocked her over suffered a similarly cut knee and a black eye. It had taken weeks to explain to Christiana one can't literally deliver an eye for an eye on a sport playing field.

Other memories flashed through his head and he knew he would add this one to the store he held deep in his heart.

His heart? his brain echoed. With a blinding flash of pain and worry, he realized they really were destined to be together, that they were True Mates. He carried her scent with him wherever he went, she was never far from his thoughts.

He would help her with anything she asked, whether it be to rob a bank or, more likely with his Christiana, to play poker against God and win.

He realized with a grimace that the Old Man was right. Zachariah Rutledge had once told him that he and Christiana were bound by strings far stronger than those binding the average pair of friends.

In his heart, Edward had understood what the Old Man meant but he had refused to believe it. But now, with her sitting above him, flushed and excited from her first real sexual experience, he knew he had his work cut out for him.

No time like the present to initiate her.

In her sitting position, her panties were barely covered by her micro miniskirt. Deciding to take advantage of that, he rolled into a kneeling position, deftly kicking his pants aside.

"Before the main course, my sweet, it's *my* turn for an appetizer, I think."

"Uh..."

Not letting her get a word in—his Christi could twist a man in circles with her woman's logic—he deftly pulled her legs out and spread them wide.

There was no need to lift her skirt—it was so short it was hitched up enough as it was. For a moment he frowned. Why the hell did his Christiana own a skirt this short?

Refusing to think down *that* pathway and into madness, he simply concentrated on pulling aside her panties. Smiling in a very masculine, knowing way, he ignored the squeak of protest from his Christi, and pulled them down and over her heels and off her legs. Folding them, he decided they would be a brilliant trophy for him later on.

The panties, he couldn't help but notice, were the palest of blue, the silk soaked in her own juices. Edward licked his lips as he gently eased them into his crumpled pants pocket, more grateful than ever for his fantastic night vision.

She smelled of desire, anticipation and his beloved friend. He would know her anywhere. What he *hadn't* known was that she shaved.

Interesting, very interesting. His Christi-girl seemed to be a woman grown now.

Leaning his head down and ignoring her gasps, he gently licked the puffy lips covering all her secrets and desires. With his tongue, he eased apart her folds to see the delicate flesh of her pussy. Licking his tongue in, he tasted her juices for the first time.

It was so sweet, so hot he couldn't help but moan in pleasure. Despite his best held efforts, in the deepest, darkest hour of the night he had often tasted her in his mind, a million times so, yet the reality was much better. Her heat flowed over him, ensnared him.

He lapped at her like he never had for a woman before. Over and over he thrust his tongue inside her as he wished he could do with his cock. In and out and in and out, over and over.

With his thumb, he stroked her clit, standing erect and crying for attention. When she tried to wriggle away from him he simply held her still with one hand, massaging her clit with his finger, and still licking her.

He thrust his tongue right up as far into her as he could reach. Lapping at her a minute, he then withdrew, causing her to groan. Circling his tongue around her hard clit, he eased one of his big, thick fingers into her wet heat. Curving and probing, he found her G-spot and ran the tip of his finger over it again and again.

She screamed and began to shudder. He continued to lick her clit, gently now, more to stimulate than anything. Rubbing her G-spot, increasing and decreasing the pressure at will, he dipped down every now and then to lap at her juices and enjoy her unique flavor.

Within moments he was hard again, desperate to plunge himself inside her and claim her, mark her as his so no other man would be stupid enough to try and get her. Deep inside himself, he knew it would be futile to try and take her now. He needed a plan, a means of convincing her they were destined.

He loved his stubborn mate but trying to convince her of anything had always been tricky. This proved to be more so than anything else.

His thoughts disintegrated as he felt Christiana begin to convulse below him. She grabbed his back, his shoulders, any part of him to keep herself steady. She smashed her pussy into his mouth, moaning and crying out from the immense pleasure he was giving her.

With a final flick of her clit and lap with his tongue, he watched as she threw her head back in abandon and screamed, long and loud, her cries echoing over the dark, empty college grounds. He growled in pleasure, with the possessive, purely masculine ego of satisfying one's chosen mate. As Christiana came down from her high, shaking and sweating lightly, her breath coming in panting snatches, he continued to lap up the last of her freely flowing juice.

She was tasty, good enough to keep him sated for a while longer, to get his patience back in control and woo her as she deserved.

He sat up and pulled his pirate shirt back over his chest.

"So what's on the menu next, Christi-girl?"

He saw the passionate haze begin to clear from his Mate's eyes. She was finally coming back to earth, the endorphins losing their grip on her.

"I think that's enough for one night, don't you? I don't know about you but my legs and nerves wouldn't stand for anything more intense."

He smiled, sad but not surprised with her reaction. His Christiana would want to step back, reassess the situation and work out how to regain the control.

"I know this won't make much difference to you right now, Christi, but sex isn't about one person being in control. Sex is two people on equal footing, both giving and both taking. You can't hope to be in control all the time. It's much easier just to accept that."

She smiled a sweet, charming smile that melted his heart. Damn, she was sweet.

"I know. But I'd much rather stay in control when it comes to you. Otherwise I'm likely to end up on the losing end again."

Unable to help himself, he reached out to touch her cheek. Gently, he stroked down her soft skin. "I'm not going to hurt you this time, Christi-girl. I just think there's a lot more for you to understand before you believe that."

She smiled and pulled away and he let her. He knew her well enough to know she needed a bit of room now.

He stood up and pulled on his thong and breeches, belting them swiftly. He concentrated on his task, giving her a minute to rearrange herself. He then held out his hand.

"Let's head back. You need some sleep before we head back home tomorrow morning."

"We?"

"Sure," he smiled, uncaring whether she could see him in the dark. "Grandpa told me to come and pick you up. Your parents are organizing your room at the house until you work out where you want to live. I'm taking you and all those stupid trunks you've packed back home."

"Oh. So we have a day's drive together in your cramped truck."

He looked at her reproachfully as they headed back to her dorm.

"The only reason it will be cramped is because of you and all those damned bags you insisted on bringing. I told you to pack light back at Christmas."

"You didn't warn me you'd be picking me up in the truck! Otherwise I'd have only packed a backpack! Nothing else will fit!"

Edward smiled. At least some things didn't change. He argued companionably back to her dorm.

When they had reached her door, once again, she surprised him.

"Give me my panties back, Edward."

He raised an eyebrow at her, knowing the masculine mockery in the gesture was sure to drive her wild.

"Finders keepers, Christi-girl."

He struggled hard not to laugh at the well-known "look-of-death" she speared him with.

"I'll wrestle you for them," she ground out, mad as fire.

Edward couldn't help himself and he laughed. "Wrestle me? With that belt you call a skirt and half the college hanging out in the corridors jeering at you? I don't think so. If you're really sweet and clever, you might be able to negotiate for them later. But who knows?" he teased her, leaning forward to taunt her more. "By then I could have done *anything* with them."

The anger and fury on her face said it all. Edward knew he had won this scuffle, and felt inordinately proud of the fact.

"You are so weird," she complained in that petulant, well-known losing voice he had heard millions of times growing up with her.

He laughed gently at her. "No, darling, I'm a fairly ordinary male. You simply haven't learned how to deal with that yet."

Refusing to give her time to realize that, if she kissed him passionately, she could steal them back herself, Edward leaned in to give her a chaste kiss good-bye. Holding the door open for her, he watched her stomp into her room and slam the door behind her.

He grinned and started whistling as he left. Relieved how well the night had gone, he smiled in joy.

Some things never change.

Chapter Twelve

ဆ

Christiana greeted Edward with a large purple and green suitcase in one hand, a backpack slung over each shoulder and a large dark red beauty case slung across her middle. He grinned at her cheerily as if he didn't even notice the armor she had been determined to erect between them.

The beast was obviously as dense as a fence post.

The beast in question stood in the doorway, a simple, tiny backpack slung over one shoulder.

Christiana frowned, diverted for a moment.

"You have two days' worth of clothes and toiletries in there? How do you men do it?"

The happy grin became more pronounced, more feral. Christiana tried not to notice how her heart thudded even harder.

"One thin, wispy pirate suit that squashes easily, plus two sets of jocks, some deodorant, a toothbrush and a razor. One small backpack, what's the big secret?"

Christiana frowned more and muttered under her breath. Pointing grumpily to the large assortment of bags and suitcases stacked by the door, she silently cursed thick-skinned and thick-headed men.

Christiana knew she was heading into trouble. She knew it from the way he brushed up against her body as he entered her small dorm, patted her ass in a dominating manner. His actions simultaneously made her teeth clench and her mouth go dry from sexual awareness,

Edward obviously didn't understand she needed a breather, needed a bit of space to sort out the turmoil currently overtaking her mind. Refusing to take her hints with the luggage and her grumpy manner before he picked up her cases, he stepped as close as possible to her and held each arm still, so she couldn't escape, and leaned in for a kiss.

Christiana felt her toes curl, her face and chest flush warmly and a trickle between her legs she refused to acknowledge. How dare the beast turn her on with a simple "Hey-there-how-you-doing" kiss?

When Edward finally pulled back, Christiana swallowed the idiotic whimper of pain she felt bubble in her throat. She would *not* become some stupid puddle of spineless woman. She was the Pack's future leader, an Alpha in her own right. She didn't need *any* man except for her True Mate, who would help her and be her strength.

Edward was just a quick fling to educate herself.

As the beast bent down to pick up her other three suitcases and two carry-on bags, she wished to hell telling herself he wasn't her True Mate over and over would work. All it seemed to do was give her a headache from thinking, not convince her he really *wasn't* her True Mate.

"This the lot, Sweet One?" he queried easily.

Christiana sighed.

"It's not like anything else will fit in your damn truck. Yes, this is the lot."

Edward grinned, and pushed her shoulder gently so she walked out of the dorm.

"I did warn you," he chided.

"You did not," she argued with some heat. "You merely ordered me in that pompous way you do to get my back up. I purposely packed more, certain you wouldn't *really* be picking me up. You know, if we're supposed to have some sort of relationship, talking to me, not ordering, will get you further."

Edward smiled as he lowered the back of the truck to make more room for her stuff.

"Talking gets me nowhere, Sweet One. With you, a man needs to be firm. I know you're the next leader and I'm happy to support and back you up with that. But you need to understand our relationship has almost nothing to do with the Pack. You need to realize that what happens between us in private has no relevance to your position of leadership there. It's between you and me."

Christiana sighed as she threw her bags onto the seat. How could Edward telling her stuff she'd already known for ages make her want to argue? *She* knew she wanted a helpmate, a man who was strong enough to let her lead the Pack but still retain his ego intact, but hearing Edward say so made her uneasy and she couldn't tell why.

"I think we'd better head on back. It's a long drive," she said, climbing into the cab. She didn't want to argue, yet she had too much pride to agree with the beast.

From the width of his smile, he knew her diversionary tactic for what it was. Since when had men become so impossible to handle?

* * * * *

Christiana stared out the window at the semi-familiar scenery passing by. She and Edward had been crammed into his midnight blue Chevy truck for nearly two hours and she was ready to scream in frustration.

All night she had tossed and turned, imagining a million scenarios. Her sitting atop Edward, both of them naked in the moonlight, her riding his cock, long and hard. Or him behind her, thrusting into her over and over and making her come time after time. Or even both of them against a tree, a desk, the walls of a nearby building—anywhere! As long as they fucked madly and freely for hours and hours and she could finally sate herself and her curiosity.

At some stage last night, whether before or after she had tasted his long, hard cock in her mouth she didn't know, her body had decided it wanted to fuck Edward raw. She was no longer sure that she could play with him and *not* try to jump his bones.

She took a deep breath as the scenery grew less and less populated. She and Edward had grown silent a short while ago, the pleasantries being exhausted and neither really needing to chatter simply to make noise.

Even though she felt perfectly comfortable in their friendship, Christiana wanted to talk about something, *anything,* so her mind could ignore the mental images of Edward thrusting himself into her mouth.

If she imagined him plunging his tongue, or other parts of his anatomy, deep inside her one more time she would come right here in the truck. And these were the non-XXX-rated fantasies intimately flashing through her mind.

"So, has anything really changed back home?"

Christiana had been disappointed, but understanding that only four members of her family could come to her college graduation. The whole event had been rained out. As the campus hall could only accommodate so many people, even ignoring the fire hazard rules, each student had only been given four tickets.

Two of Christiana's siblings and her parents had arrived, leaving her with a million questions on how things at home were going. Email and phone calls were fine, but not like personal contact.

Christiana glanced at Edward as he concentrated on the roads and updated her on what was going on in her family's life. Edward and his parents had been taken under her Grampa Zachariah's wing. Even though they weren't actually family, they were considered as such. They lived in the woods, where Roland, Edward's father, could run when he felt the need.

Edward talked about the security company her father, Artemais, ran. He told her how he had grown bored with working the business side of things and had joined up with her Uncles Dominic and Samuel in the investigative side of the business. Edward went onto explain how he and Matthew, also a member of their extended family, and her Aunts Mary and Chloe's only other relative, had begun plans to open their own sideline in the investigative and security businesses.

Edward explained how tracking people and keeping up-to-date with all the security measures more than fulfilled him, keeping his active mind and fingers busy. With something new to do every day he felt not only useful, but like all his talents were appreciated.

Edward finally moved on from his gushing over work to how her cousins and siblings were faring at their different colleges and traineeships. While her rather large family was spread out everywhere, everyone always made it home for Christmas and most of them did their best to make it to the weekends for special birthdays.

Christiana interrupted every now and then, asking questions and trying to get some clarification on different things. While she kept in regular email contact with most of her family, it was never the same thing as talking to them face-to-face or laughing and pulling pranks with them.

The time slipped away. They ate drive-thru food, laughing over shared jokes and old memories. The years just seemed to slip away and the camaraderie and friendship they had always seemed to hold fell back into place, as if they had spent the past five years laughing together such as this.

Before she knew it they were driving through the nearest village, where lots of her childhood friends had grown up. Many members of the Pack lived and worked here. A number of the older members had passed away, their children either moving away or growing apart.

Christiana found herself looking forward to coming home, even if she would be moving away once she started working in the city with her father's company. The nearly two hour long drive would be nothing compared to the long haul from college. It would be nice to be home for a change.

* * * * *

"You *what*?!"

Edward felt his face harden into almost a mask. He knew Artemais Rutledge cared for him practically as a member of his family. He had no qualms about welcoming him into their ancestral home, no problems with him working in the family firm.

Yet on the subject of Christiana, apparently he would be treated the same as any other man. Deciding it wiser to be more formal, he repeated his "request".

"I said, Sir, that I am requesting Christiana's hand in marriage. I believe we are True Mates and wish to mate with her."

"You are kidding me?!"

Despite the way the man bellowed, Edward did not move. He felt if a fight broke out, it wouldn't last long simply because both Christiana and her mother, Sophie, were only downstairs.

The older man stood up from his chair and paced over to where Edward stood. Face-to-face, he could feel the rage vibrating from the older man.

"If you tell me she's pregnant with your child, I'll…"

With so much anger vibrating, begging to be let loose from Artemais, Edward decided not to tease the old guy.

"Of course she's not pregnant. She's still a virgin. She doesn't believe us to be mates. I was merely informing you of my intentions, both as a respected friend and the father of the woman I plan to marry, as well as my Pack Alpha. You know I respect both you and Christiana. Do you really think I'd force her, or that she'd let me be here alone if she had an inkling of what I was doing?"

Most of the anger left Artemais.

"You have a point there, son." He crossed over to the sideboard and poured a Scotch for himself and Edward. Edward cleared his throat and decided it was time to lighten the mood.

"Besides, from what I hear, the scenario you're so deathly afraid of here is exactly how you and Sophie came together."

Artemais handed him a glass and smiled sappily. "Yeah, that's right. I just don't want to see my baby put in that situation."

The study door opened and Zachariah entered the room. "What's all this fuss about? Can't a man nap in the evenings anymore?"

Both Artemais and Edward smiled.

"Gramps," Artemais started, "Edward here was just battling me for rights over Christiana. Seems the boy might even be able to manage that girl of mine."

The Old Man snorted. "'Course he can—what do you think I've been trying to point out to all and sundry all these years?"

Edward came forward and helped the Old Man into one of the large, leather-padded chairs. Frowning, he looked down at the ancient wolf.

"Gramps, why have you been so determined to bring us together? It's never been anything truly overt but everyone knows your feelings on the matter."

Zachariah looked from his eldest grandson to the man he had helped raise from a pup. Sighing, he ran a hand through his thin hair. Despite his age and wrinkles, his eyes were still sharp, as was his brain.

"Sit down lad, this might take a bit of time. Years and years ago, your Grandma, your dad's mom, was a member of our Pack. Back in those days, we had the equivalent of medicine men who would sniff out the young lads and lasses and match the True-Mated pairs. It's all in the scent, in the ability to mingle a man and woman's scent. If their scent won't mingle, then not only can't they have children, but neither can they join their lives together. It's as simple and complex as that.

"Your Grandma didn't want to marry the man she was to be joined with. She had fallen in love with a half-human werewolf from a neighboring Pack. This wasn't a bad thing in its own but our medicine man had stated his scent was wrong—not just for her, but for his own life's sake. Your Grandma refused to listen and I was forced to make a decision. Either exile her, or force her to do the Pack's traditional will.

"I sat down with her, explained the reservations the medicine man held, tried to reason with her. But she was young and in love and refused to listen. Eventually we agreed that I would exile her but she would have enough time to pack up her things and ready herself to leave. Neither of us was truly happy with the arrangement but it was the best we could come up with.

"As you know, your father was born of the union, but at a great personal cost. The man who fathered him was mentally ill, deranged. He not only killed his entire tiny pack, but much of our own. We had no real concept of syphilis. We were still following many of the old traditions before the culling.

"And so I felt a huge burden of guilt. I had loved Janine like I loved everyone in the Pack, yet I couldn't help feeling if I had just been stronger, more forceful, maybe I could have helped her avoid all that agony and grief her chosen mate had put her and her baby, your father, through.

"And so I set out to help her son. I felt if I could heal Roland, help him become the man he really was, that, in some respect, would help ease my burden, atone for the sins I had unwittingly committed. But there was more. I knew in my heart that Janine's line was supposed to be joined to our line. I even knew it when the old medicine man, who had died in the culling, had set her up with another man. I had no substance to back up my claim...yet when I saw you, as a tiny infant, I knew you were the key. Knew you could right all those old wrongs for me. I knew you and Artemais' eldest child could fix the past. But my interference had already caused enough damage. So I let it lie.

"But, it's nice to see an old man's crazy schemes come into fruition."

Edward stared in shock, his Scotch completely forgotten in his hand. This was easily the longish speech he had ever heard from Zachariah, a man of few words.

"I have to convince *her* first."

Artemais chuckled, almost choking on his Scotch. "Well, son, I wish you the best of luck. I don't think anyone but you has *ever* been able to convince that girl of anything. You've set yourself up for a big task, but you have my blessing, for what it's worth."

Edward smiled hugely. "That's all I was looking for, as I think you know. I didn't want to suddenly invite you to the wedding and have to face the four of you over pistols at dawn or something."

Artemais handed Zachariah a glass of Scotch and refilled his own and Edward's.

"I propose a toast. To Edward and his convincing skills on my beloved Christiana."

Edward raised his glass and drank deeply. He'd certainly drink to that! He'd need all the help he could get.

* * * * *

Christiana heard her dad bellow something—the words were indistinguishable through the heavy walls but the bellowing roar was easy to understand—and exchanged a glance with her mom.

Sophie Rutledge looked supremely unconcerned about the noise coming from her husband's study.

"Give them five minutes. If we hear the furniture begin to break or more noise we'll go in and stop them. Otherwise it might be best to give them their space."

Christiana was going to argue until she heard the creak of her Grandfather's door open and him shuffling down the hall, muttering curses.

Grampa would keep everything in line.

She turned back to her mom, bemused to find she had instantly turned back to peeling the potatoes for dinner. It was comforting but slightly alarming how some things never changed.

"So what are your plans, my girl?"

Christiana sat back and smiled.

"I'm not sure, Mom. I'll stay here 'til I get an apartment down in the city. And I plan to start working full time with Dad in the day-to-day aspects of the business but I really want to sorta shift around until I find an area of interest. There's sure to be something in the company that appeals to me."

Her mother nodded.

Christiana fidgeted. She picked up a peeler and helped start in on the potatoes.

"What's on your mind, hon?"

Christiana instantly thought of a dozen blow-offs—and then instantly cast them aside. It would be no use trying to deter her mother. She had *always* had the ability to read her like a book.

"It's Edward, Mom."

Nodding, Sophie waited, patiently.

"He's annoying! He seduces me one minute and then makes me mad as fire the next! He can never decide exactly what he wants and, then as soon as I turn my back, he's hounding me again!"

Sophie smiled. "We had a conversation just like this when you were about fourteen, didn't we, dear?"

Christiana resisted the impulse to throw the peeler onto the bench and pout. "This is different!" she insisted.

"How so, love?"

Christiana opened her mouth, and then shut it again. Then she opened it, but shut it again.

Sophie continued to peel the potatoes, obviously not in a rush.

"This time we're adults, Mom," she started very, very softly. "This time I want to believe we're destined, I want to believe that I can turn my very oldest, best friend into the lover of my lifetime. I don't think I could bear to be broken-hearted again."

Sophie smiled slightly, but didn't raise her eyes from the potato she was peeling. "And so?"

"So what?" she questioned, confused.

"Well, what do *you* think he's doing in your father's study that has him bellowing like a wounded bear, bashing his very old, very expensive mahogany desk?"

Christiana stopped peeling, frowning. "I thought Edward was just talking to Dad?"

"He is, but you're supposed to be smarter than this, dear. What do you think they're talking about?"

Christiana found her mouth falling open. "He's not...? He wouldn't...? He's doing the *traditional* thing and asking Dad...? But what about my opinion??!! What about MY choice??! *Why the hell isn't he asking ME?!*"

Sophie continued peeling the potatoes, a huge grin breaking out on her face. Christiana ignored the innate knowledge that her mom had known all along what was going on, and simply had been holding her mirth in check.

Christiana very carefully placed her peeler on the bench and stood up so she could pace furiously.

"Ooh!!! I'm going to kill him! Tear him apart! How *dare* he ask my father before even talking to me! Who the hell does he think he is?"

"Don't wear out my tiles, love. How about you start thinking smart, instead of angry?"

Christiana stopped, determined not to snap at her mom. "Well, what would *you* do, Mom?"

"Oh, that's easy. Obviously, Edward would want to be in control. If he's getting your father's blessing, then he plans to move fairly quickly. Why not beat him to the punch? Surely there's something special between the two of you—some sort of sexual game or sexual initiative you could take that you would both enjoy?"

Christiana thought of the pirate outfit Edward probably still had packed away in his backpack from their long trek back from college. She frowned as she realized she might have actually brought it into her own room with the mountain of other bags and luggage she had.

She couldn't recall Edward carrying his own backpack anywhere. He had dumped her larger trunks into her room and headed for her dad's office. More than likely she had picked his backpack up with all her other smaller things and dumped them somewhere...

Her mom was a decent seamstress and, with her help and a bit of patience, she would be able to fit it easily with a few modifications. Where the hell had she stashed that mask she had removed from him... Thinking so hard, she barely caught her mother's next brainwave.

"Take him somewhere secluded and live out your fantasies, my dear. It's about time you had some real fun."

Christiana stalked over to the phone. Pulling open her old high school telephone book, she started dialing numbers. Finally, she hit paydirt.

"Yeah? You serious? And I can pick up the keys right now? I can be over there in about twenty minutes. Thanks, Billy, I definitely owe you one."

Hanging up the phone, she grinned at her mother. "Just borrowing the car for a bit. Gotta pick up keys from Billy's place. Can I borrow fifty bucks 'til I hit an ATM?"

Sophie nodded to where her purse lay on the table. "Have fun, dear."

Christiana thought of the pirate costume and grinned. She had a gorgeous black, sparkly bra and matching G-string that would go perfectly with the costume. Edward wouldn't know what hit him.

"Oh, I will, Mom. I will."

With that she snagged the keys and headed out the door.

Chapter Thirteen

Edward groaned and woke up with a slight headache. He had always known he couldn't sleep with Christiana while they were at her parents' place. But somehow it all seemed that much harder now that he knew how this True Mate business worked and he had Artemais' permission to be with her.

He instinctively tried to roll over and found his arms bound behind him. Blinking, he found himself rapidly waking up. Before he could shake all the fog from his head, though, he felt a gag being placed in his mouth.

Edward squirmed into a position he could lever himself upright into, but found himself enveloped in Christiana's scent. He froze, totally confused, and still a bit sleepy.

"Ahoy there, matey," she whispered in his ear, the soft tone of her voice making her sound sleepy and husky and like sex incarnate. He twisted, turned so he could get a look at her, and nearly toppled over in lust.

She was wearing his damned pirate suit! That little vixen had stolen his act!

Even amid his outrage, he had to admit the costume looked far more enticing on Christiana. He had bought the first costume that fitted him from the shop. Now he had a much higher appreciation for the silky outfit. The silky shirt billowed around her leaner frame. She had tied it underneath her impressive cleavage, a sparkly black bra playing peek-a-boo with her creamy flesh underneath the severe black.

The breeches were fantastic. They were see-through enough to cause a scene and get the imagination, not to mention other body parts, going, but still opaque enough that he could only catch glimpses of her lightly muscled, slender legs.

The mental pictures of how she had changed, but still remained the same Christiana he knew so well as a child, made his mouth water and his cock harden. Try as he might, he couldn't see whether she wore a thong or not. The question of whether she was bare or simply wearing a skimpy thong did things to his cock he had no right feeling while bound and gagged.

For a moment, he couldn't tell if he was dreaming or if she really was stringing kisses down along his neck and chest. Her soft, silky golden curls caught the light from the moon filtering in through the curtains. Edward had never thought of Christiana taking control of him sexually like this but his brain, not to mention his cock, didn't seem to have any arguments with the scene.

Gagged, he couldn't do anything other than moan. He desperately wished his hands were free to push her toward his achingly aroused shaft. All too soon she lifted herself back up to look in his face.

"Sorry about that, matey, couldn't resist. I'm supposed to be the one in control here but something about your delicious body just screams out to me. I'd better get this show on the road before you work out a way to disarm me."

He grunted in agreement and disappointment as Christiana used her strength as a werewolf and half-lifted him off the bed, helping him onto his bound feet.

"Aren't you glad I insisted you sleep on the ground floor? I won't have to carry you to my little Geo Metro. "

Edward snorted beneath his gag. He knew Christiana was physically fit enough and, as a werewolf, strong enough to carry him outside to the car. What she obviously hadn't thought about was *he* was strong enough to break these ropes and stop the fun if she *dared* try to carry him around like some damned baby.

Luckily for them both he could hobble with her help into the damned tiny car.

She helped him inside it, safely buckling him into the passenger seat, still tied up. He was privately wondering just how far he should let her get away with this, until she started pulling a blindfold over his eyes.

He pulled away, determined to fight this last bit.

"Oh fine then! But don't blame me if you feel sick at being bound in the car while I drive. I was only trying to make the trip easier for you. We won't be driving for long," she continued, knowing him well enough to answer the one burning question in his mind, "just down to the village, thirty minutes tops."

He grunted and sat back. Thirty minutes of torture would be okay to try and see through those damn breeches and work out if she wore anything underneath them. And who knows, her own seat belt might make the pirate shirt look damn good, too — if it spread enough to give him an eyeful of cleavage.

Edward sat back, turned toward her. Even so, it would still be a long thirty minutes.

Chapter Fourteen

ରୁ

Christiana tried desperately to concentrate on the road ahead of her, and not the bound stud next to her. Who would have guessed having a studly man bound and gagged could be *such* a turn-on?

Smiling, remembering some of the games Ian and Maggie used to play together, she figured maybe everyone *except* her had realized what a turn-on it was.

Even concentrating on the road, half her mind was focusing on Edward, seated next to her as he alternated between staring at her and silently fuming. Thankfully, she knew this road better than she knew her own face in the mirror. They made the short trip to the remote cabin just on the outskirts of the village in decent time.

Christiana parked the car and got out to help Edward. Hobbling again, they made short work of the few feet to the small veranda. Christiana fumbled with the keys, swearing under her breath, and they made a lot of noise stumbling into the cabin.

Christiana was grateful she had already made this trip once tonight before dinner to set everything up. She knew Edward's patience and tolerance would only extend so far. When he worked out that she had no intention of letting him free any time soon, his limited patience would probably snap, along with his temper.

As they were well secluded within the woods and no one would disturb them for ages, Christiana left the door open to air the tiny cabin out a bit. Still helping Edward hobble in, she casually led him over to the huge bed that took up most of the cabin's interior, and sat him down on the edge.

She didn't turn-on the lamp, partially because she didn't need the light as she knew the layout of the cabin, but also partially because she didn't want Edward looking too closely at the bed.

She removed his gag first, hoping to make him feel more comfortable, but also so he would think she would be releasing him soon.

Silly man.

"You know," he started amiably after she had removed the gag, "that was one hell of a trick, stealing my costume and turning the tables on me. I must remember that one for the future."

She smiled and pushed him back gently. "Yes indeed, I was rather proud of it myself."

Carefully, so as to not alert him to her true intentions, she unbound his hands. As he flexed his wrists, rubbing them gently to ease the soreness out of his muscles, she straddled him, pinning him on the bed without arousing his suspicions.

He grabbed her ass as she sat on top of him and laughed.

"Is this where you take advantage of me and start that pirate's method of raping and pillaging?"

"Rape? Aren't you willing?" she teased, knowing full well from the steel of his cock pressing against her exactly what his thoughts on the matter were.

"Of course I am, Sweet One. I'm hard as a bone thinking of finally getting deep, deep inside you. You have no idea how long I've been waiting for this."

Smiling, Christiana grabbed his hands in her own, and lifted them above his head.

"You have *no* idea how much I needed to hear that. So you're willing to play my little games?" she teased, hoping he wouldn't understand just how serious she was.

"Of course," he laughed, oblivious.

Quickly, using all her dexterity, she released his wrists and snapped the fur-lined handcuffs her mother had loaned her around his thick wrists. She groaned mentally at the thought of her mom and dad playing with these... Maybe she should confiscate them on principle after she was finished with them!

"What the...? Christi-girl, this had better damn well be a joke!"

Not knowing exactly how to soothe the wounded beast, Christiana leaned forward and kissed him with all her pent-up passion. Years and years of suppressed desire, worries and teenage angst came pouring out as she released her passion for Edward.

Soon, he was returning her hungry, inquisitive kiss with a most demanding one of his own. He tilted his hips up into her, demanding attention for his iron-hard cock.

Seeing as she had stopped short of his cock earlier in the evening, and he now really *was* bound and at her mercy, she relented and figured he would be more amiable if she gave him some of what he wanted.

Relieved she only had to pull the slipknot around his feet to free him, Christiana settled herself so her face was just in front of his erect shaft.

She slowly stroked his cock, first with her fingers, then with her tongue, relearning the rigid lengths of it, silently promising it close attention in the near future. Not this time, but next, she mentally promised it.

"Damn, Christi-girl, you'd better take me inside you soon. After the bumpy ride you made down here, where any cop could have pulled us over and asked about your naked prisoner, you owe me, Sweet One."

Pulling away from Edward's enticing cock, she sat up, undulating her bottom against him, taunting him further.

"Christiana," he groaned, "this really isn't the best time to tease me—I'm more likely to break this damn bed than these stupid cuffs. I really don't want to be driven mad before your first time. I'd rather go slow for your sake."

Christiana smiled and began to inch the pirate shirt up her chest.

"Now Edward, who said anything about slow? I've had years to prepare myself. I know more about my own body than you currently do—though I am hoping to change that status over the next few hours. What say you let me deal with my virginity in my own way and *then* we can talk?"

With that, she pulled the silk shirt totally off, showcasing a tiny demi-bra, black with sparkly beads and sequins sewn onto the cups.

The chilly night wind caused her nipples to pucker, though thankfully that reaction was hidden behind her bra. The dampness in her crotch, however, was given away through the thinness of the pirate pants and her almost-non-existent thong.

Christiana, however, was too interested in Edward and his reactions to be worried about her own.

Edward stared at her, mouth agape, and Christiana smiled. Between the sweat beading on his forehead, the heaving pants of his chest and the iron-hard cock between her legs, she felt quite satisfied with her work so far. *This* was the sort of reaction she was looking for.

She shimmied against his groin, causing him to moan and groan like a man in mortal pain. Inch by inch, she let the breeches slide down her legs, until she had to reach down, slipping her sandals off and pulling the pants free from her legs.

"Oh shit, a man can't take too much of this," he complained, staring at her matching G-string. A tiny triangle of black silk, with shiny beads sewn into the material to make it shimmer and call a man to his doom.

Once again he was reminded of one of the important answers to life. Christiana definitely shaved. The lips of her pussy pouted, free and clear of any hair. A light sprinkling of hair dusted her mons, just enough to tempt and tease a man dying from unexplored lust.

Christiana held still above him for a moment, letting him take in as much as he could. Men were, after all, visual creatures.

When she feared for his sanity—she did not want a drooling moron for a lover—she bent down and kissed him once more. Sliding her tongue into his mouth, she tasted her Edward. He was so familiar, even though they had not kissed much. It was as if she had always known his taste, his scent. She wasn't surprised but it was comforting, sweet.

Deciding she couldn't wait much longer, sitting happily over his cock, she started to wiggle her G-string down her thighs. As she flipped the scrap of material off the edge of the bed, she twisted her arms back, intending to unclasp her demi-bra.

"No!" he cried out. "Leave the bra on! It's kind of a turn-on. It sparkles like your eyes."

Rolling her eyes at the strange notions of men, Christiana nevertheless left the bra on. Rubbing her dripping pussy over the long length of his cock, she felt her own mouth start to drool. For years she had fantasized about this moment. She could barely believe that she was finally here.

The moon shone in through the window, bathing them in Her light. Her lover, the man of her fantasies and dreams, lay before her, ready and eager to do her bidding. Sure, she knew as soon as she removed the handcuffs he would exact his revenge, but how sweet that would also be. Her mouth watered at all the things he might do to her, might make her do to *him*.

Running her swollen, dripping pussy lips over and over his cock, she unconsciously set up a rhythm. She didn't mean to set up the thrusting, grinding pace but it was more instinctual than that. But Edward immediately caught on and began to thrust his hips in synch to her rhythm.

"Now, Christi! I need you now!"

Eagerly agreeing, she changed her angle and thrust herself down on his dripping cock. Her own juices had coated him—something she was grateful for, even though that hadn't been her intention.

She felt her hymen tear, a most unusual feeling, and then he was simply *there*. It wasn't unpleasant but it was too uncomfortable to be precisely *pleasant*. She felt full, and the feeling was weird, almost shocking.

She panted, realizing that Edward was panting, too.

"I *told* you I should have helped you with this. I could have made it easier. Stroke your clit, darling. Give yourself some pleasure to counteract the pain."

"It's not exactly pain, Edward." But even as she spoke, she began to stroke herself, surprised at how much it eased the uncomfortable feeling. "I'm just a bit full at the moment."

"A bit?" he teased. "Sweetheart, you ain't seen nothin' yet."

With that, he began to thrust in and out of her with a slow, steady rhythm.

The friction of his cock made tingles with the friction of her finger stroking her clit. Soon, she felt herself relaxing around his cock, even thrusting in tangent with him, eager to feel him deeper.

She opened her eyes, unaware of when she had closed them, to find Edward staring at her, his eyes burning in the darkness. He had turned the cuffs slightly, so he gripped them with an iron grip, using them as leverage to thrust his body deeper and deeper inside her.

It was strangely erotic. Maybe it was simply the heat and intensity of his eyes, the love and lust and need she saw in those depths.

She moaned, the desire and pent-up need she felt vibrating through his body driving her wild.

She felt something building inside her. It was so much larger than her own, private orgasms. This was huge, building like a giant wave about to crash over her. She let it come, knowing from her private experience that if one fought an orgasm, one lost it.

She opened to it, let Edward thrust deeper and deeper inside her as she stroked her clit, pushed herself back onto him, grinding their bodies together.

And then suddenly she threw her head back and screamed. There was no other way to release the tension inside herself. She screamed and felt her body closing vise-like around his immense shaft. She felt the ripples cascade through her and her clit became ultrasensitive and she almost stopped stroking it.

The convulsions racked through her body and she finally began to fall from the high.

She came back to earth, slowly and carefully. She felt sure she had a sappy, post-orgasmic stupid look on her face. All her girlfriends had told her it was so. It took her a moment to realize Edward hadn't come. Edward was looking a little better, but still very hot and bothered and, if the giant cock still rammed up inside her was any indication, he was far from finished.

She silently wondered what she had gotten herself into.

Chapter Fifteen

℘

Edward watched Christiana come down from her orgasm and felt a fierce surge of possessiveness wash through him.

She was his now. No matter what she said or did, she was his. He knew this wasn't her first orgasm but it was damn well her first orgasm with a man inside her and so it was the first one that counted.

He had felt the rending tear as he had pierced her hymen. Never having had a virgin, he hadn't been aware that a man could feel it yet he had. Somehow it had made everything even more intense. In the second he had felt that tear, everything had cemented for him.

They were perfect together and they both knew it. His Christi-girl might need a bit more time, and undoubtedly a lot more convincing, but he *knew* they were meant to be.

The tear had touched him, also. He had never questioned that Christiana had stayed pure—hell, she had turned him down enough that he *knew* what she would have been like to other men.

Yet, feeling that membrane tear had touched something inside him. Made him more determined than ever to make sure this was the best first experience any woman could have.

His Christiana deserved the best.

And so he had driven her up that first peak, watched her climax splendidly and held himself in check.

He was going to drag this out as long as possible for her.

He saw the glint in her gaze the second she realized he hadn't come. When she bent forward slightly, to drive him even deeper inside him, he groaned. He *hoped* to make this last longer for her. If she tried to drive him wild, however…well, a guy could only wait so long.

When she began moving up and down on him with a vengeance, he found himself pleading without even realizing it.

"Christi, I want to make this last for you…don't rush it!"

She smiled and bent down to kiss him. As she slid her tongue between his lips and then sucked his own tongue into her mouth, he moaned, totally lost. He felt himself drowning, falling deeper and deeper into her spell. He could *feel* his balls rise, ready to blow their load as soon as he let himself go.

He held on, grimly determined to let her come at least once more. He moved his hand, forgetting the cuffs for a moment. He pulled his mouth away from hers.

"Touch yourself, baby, and let me watch you come again as I shoot myself in you, *please.*"

She lifted herself up again, looking magnificent in the dark cabin. Her hair was curling and sticking in spots down her back, in the sweat *he* had created. Her demi-bra shone and sparkled at him but, best of all, her eyes were that deep, dark blue he had always loved, always lost himself in. She stared down at him as if he were the only man in the world and, for her, he was.

She rammed him deeper and deeper inside her slender body. Frantically, she toyed with her clit, both sensitive and unbearably aroused at the same time. Edward could feel the urgency inside her, could feel the gathering climax inside himself.

"Play with your breasts, baby," he commanded, amazed that she didn't even question him, but dipped both her hands inside the demi-bra, cupping both of the globes he coveted like mad, and toyed with her nipples.

This was masculine power, Edward knew. This electric sexual bond between them, the shift and flow of power and sexual chemistry, feeding from one to the other.

Edward gasped deep lungfuls of air, determined not to come until Christiana had come again. He thanked the Goddess as he felt her contracting once more around him, pushed his head back deep into the pillow and felt his control finally snap.

As they both cried out together, their mutual orgasm rocketing along with both their cries, Edward had a flash. It was like a dream—or as if an angel had handed him an instant-snap photo.

It was he and Christiana, looking out toward him. And in his Christi's arms lay the most perfect baby in existence. A tiny little girl, with his rich, dark curls, but with Christi's perfect blue eyes. She looked around six months old and she was wiggling her arms and legs excitedly, obviously wanting to be put down.

And in that same instant that he saw it, it was gone. He felt his cock explode and his seed, his very essence and his soul's passion, surged deep inside his love, his True Mate.

He cried out, both with the explosive release, and also with joy and thanksgiving deep in his soul. He blinked away the tears that had sprung up from nowhere and he enjoyed the most satisfying release of his life.

Some of his joy and happiness must have transferred over to Christiana, because he felt her come again, hard on the heels of her last orgasm, and his cock kept on and on exploding, as if he would never get enough.

Finally, she collapsed on top of him, so spent and sated she didn't even giggle at the funny noises their sweaty bodies made as they slapped together.

He let them both catch their breath, stunned both by the intensity of their first time—he shuddered at the mental images of how fantastic sex between them would be with some practice—and his joy and shock at that strange image.

"Well, now you gotta marry me. You're pregnant."

Christiana frowned, her mind obviously struggling for some reason to deny him one more time. "Don't be silly. We're both Alphas. You know only a True Mate can impregnate another Alpha. And besides, how the hell do *you* know? I thought intuition was a woman's thing."

Edward shrugged. "I thought the New Age man was supposed to have some sort of intuition. Besides, the whole True Mate concept is tricky."

Briefly, he explained what Zachariah had told him about True Mates and how it was partly destiny, but also partly luck in their scents meshing.

"But our scents…" Christiana trailed off, unsure and obviously thinking. Edward chortled.

"Oh please, our scents have been mingled since we were tiny. Why do you think Grandpa threw us together so much?"

Christiana's eyes widened. "Why that sneaky matchmaker. He's wanted this since the start, hasn't he?"

Edward shrugged, not prepared to go into it all just now. Let her work out she was pregnant first. Then they could marry—as soon as she uncuffed him he would mark her—and then everything would fall into place.

He sighed contentedly as Christiana snuggled into him. "Hey," he mumbled as a thought struck him. "Where's my mask?"

"Oh, I left it in my room. It was just too sexy and masculine to use. I figured you could use it afterwards—when we go back to pack."

"Pack?"

"Sure, if we're going to get married, then we'll have to find a house in the city."

Edward nodded and added in his two cents. Damned if he'd let her rule him completely, a man had to have his pride. "Lots of room. I want a heap of kids."

Christiana wrinkled her nose. "I dunno... You've watched that tape of Uncle Samuel's, the one of mom giving birth to me. I can't blame her for refusing to allow him to tape any of the other kids. It all looks rather undignified to me."

Edward grinned. "Oh, that's okay. You've got nine months to work on it."

Christiana raised an eyebrow and refused to comment on the obvious.

"You better ask really nicely if you want to get out before tomorrow morning."

Edward smiled and leered at her. "Pretty, pretty please with chocolate on top. May I go now, ma'am?"

Christiana laughed. "Well, if you insist," she said, digging into her bra for the key.

As she unlocked him, he promptly turned her over and started nibbling her neck, marking her. Five minutes later, when they were both straining together and panting like crazy, he pulled back, letting his sweat-soaked forehead rest on hers.

"Aha! Now you're mine!" he panted.

Christiana squirmed, but didn't really try to get away. As he lapped the spot where he had marked her, she laughed and squirmed but what was the use of running from the one place she had always wanted to be?

She laughed. Everything was just fine.

* * * * *

"Come running with me," a husky, sexy voice whispered in her ear. Christiana snuggled deeper into the warmth of the blankets and masculine arms and chest she was entwined with.

"Cold," she murmured. The chest her face pressed against rumbled with deep laughter.

"It won't be cold and you know it. Come on, Sweet One. I have this incredible urge to run with you again, like we did back when we were kids."

The light pinch to her ass had her yelping and lifting her head, opening her eyes blearily.

"It's in the middle of the night," she complained teasingly.

When Edward dragged himself from beneath the covers he shivered only slightly, naked in the chill night air. Christiana pouted slightly at the small warm spot he left in the bed where he had lain. Damn it, but she'd have to follow him now. Without his large, heated presence the bed would cool fairly quickly.

The feral grin Edward gave her let her know he knew the exact train of her thoughts.

"Come on, Sweet One," he chided, "Come run with me."

With that, her large pirate, her True Mate, shimmered and, with the blink of an eye, Changed into a huge black beast of a wolf.

Christiana sighed and dramatically pulled herself, naked, from the bed. Standing straight and tall, in no way intimidated by her naked state, she wagged her finger.

"This is bribery or emotional blackmail or something my too-tired brain can't think of." She placed her hands on her hips, confident her wolf knew exactly what she spoke. When he came and nuzzled her hips and thigh, his wet nose jolted her. She sighed.

"Fine, fine. Lets go run then. I suppose the exercise will do us both good."

With barely a thought, she shimmered and Changed.

Looking out of her wolf's eyes, Christiana found herself momentarily wondering how she could have ever doubted Edward was her True Mate. He complimented her in every area. He would be a strong mate, a rock of strength for her throughout the years to come. He would never stand between her and the Pack, yet he was confident enough to deal with her as equals in their home.

Christiana knew he saw a much lighter colored wolf, a mixture of her father's brown and her mother's blonde hair. Her blue eyes shone with happiness in the light from the moon.

With an impatient snap at his heels, she tagged him in their old manner from childhood, nudged the slightly-open cabin door wide open and ran out into the woods. A game of Chase was what he wanted?

He was "It" now and he damn well knew it. Now she just had to try and escape.

Laughing inside herself, she let the scents and sounds of the night wrap around her. She would never escape Edward, never leave him or have to question him. He might let her wander around for a while but she knew he would always be just a step behind her.

As the large wolf pounded on her from a tree ahead of her, she laughed.

Or maybe a step ahead of her. Who knew with Edward? He had always seemed a step ahead of her when she thought him a step behind.

At least he'd always keep her on her toes, she knew as she watched him dart into the trees deep in the woods.

Scenting him on the wind she gave chase. She'd catch up to him, always.

Chapter Sixteen
Six weeks later

જી

Christiana hugged her father for the fourth time in as many minutes. Feeling rather weary, she pulled from his possessive, fatherly embrace and handed him her last tissue from her purse as he tried to sniff away his tears of happiness.

"Honestly, dad, you'd think I was moving to Australia or something. I'm going to be less than an hour away, and seeing you most workdays. Not to mention evenings when I need some cooking tips from mom or when I want a moonlit romp in the backyard…"

Sophie came up to rescue her from decking her father and hugged her again.

"Really, Artemais, give the girl a chance to talk to her other guests. I thought it was the mother of the bride who is supposed to take over everything. So far I've been allowed to organize the food for the reception and nothing else. Go and talk to your brothers, beat your chests or drink some beer or something, but leave the poor girl alone."

Christiana hugged her mom as her father stalked off muttering, and whispered in her ear, "Please keep him away from me. You'd think I was going to the guillotine, not moving in with my new husband."

Sophie patted her on the back, as if she were a baby with gas and not a fully grown, newly married young woman.

"Don't worry, dear. It's just taking him a bit of time to come to terms with the fact his eldest baby is grown and mated. These things take time."

Christiana smiled. "Think I should drop the bombshell that he's about to become a grandpa?"

Sophie snickered. "You might want to save that one for a few days. You can't possibly remember what a bear he is to be with when he's in protective-baby mode. Think of how he's been the last few weeks and magnify it tenfold at least. I bet he still has some of those damn books we got when I found out about you. The man is a walking encyclopedia when it comes to pregnancy and baby tidbits."

Christiana wrinkled her nose. "Edward is the same. He's bought every book the local store has on prenatal care and pregnancy-for-dummies. He's insisting I eat the required amount of folate and calcium and he jeers at all my cravings. He doesn't believe a sundae with fries is normal for me."

Sophie frowned. "Where is Edward?"

Before Christiana had a chance to look around the small gathering of her wedding, a large pirate paced toward her.

Well-known and well-loved black curls bobbed in the sunshine and dark eyes flashed lovingly at her. Thin, black, almost-but-not-quite-see-through breeches ruffled in the slight breeze. Christiana noted the gold threading on the side, where he must have had help fixing them up after she had "altered" them.

"I'm sorry, mom," she laughed as she recognized the evil glint in her new husband's eyes. She had seen it any number of times in the last six weeks. Something, however, told her he wouldn't be sidetracked this time. Nothing on earth would stop him now they had exchanged vows. "I'm not sure I'm going to make it to the reception."

Christiana only half paid attention to her mom's sigh of resignation. As Edward swept her into his large, strong arms, she dimly heard her father pull her mother aside and whisper fiercely, "Our baby was *not* just talking to you about being pregnant, was she, Soph?"

Christiana snickered. She had forgotten how good werewolf hearing could be on occasion. Her father in particular had a radar for her and her siblings. Leaning in to her True Mate, her soul's love, she whispered into his ear, "You sure I'm not too heavy? Bub might object to being carried about like this."

"Our little girl will deal with it. She's going to be a feisty little thing. Between your pigheadedness and my stubborn streak and both of our tempers, she's going to have us and all your uncles at her beck and call. Besides, my ego needs the boost. I've had your uncles hovering over me like maiden aunts, giving me dire warnings and, if your dad reads me one more lecture, I'm likely to puke. We need to get away for a while and I figured only a Pirate would be allowed to do so."

Christiana laughed.

"I had wondered where he had gone to these last few weeks." Kissing him on the ear, nuzzling his cheek and neck, she murmured, "I missed him."

"He's back," Edward promised as he gently placed her in his truck, "back and he'll never be far away again, though we might need to invest in new pirate breeches. I have a feeling these will never be the same after your altering them. This is the start of the rest of our lives, Christi-girl. I figure we need to start it right. With me being the pirate, and you the willing captive."

Christiana smiled, grateful she had packed her handcuffs in her purse, just in case.

A girl could never be too prepared.

She leaned over and continued to nuzzle Edward as he started the truck. She didn't even think to ask him where they were going. They were together and that was all that counted in her mind.

Like the true pirate he was, Edward drove them away into the hills, one arm on the wheel of the car, one arm around his Mate.

He wanted this time between them to be special. Their little girl would be diverting their attention soon enough. Not to mention his explanations to Artemais and his brothers. Zachariah Rutledge had urged him to do this and he had been profoundly grateful for the Old Man's assistance in packing all the gear the two of them might need.

But he could see, could *feel,* how happy Christiana was to be here with him so everything else would work itself out.

Edward smiled as they drove off into the woods.

Epilogue
ഔ

Zachariah leaned back from the window. The newest addition to his family lay screaming up a storm in the garden outside his ancestral home. Margaret Naomi Rose Rutledge Matthews was beginning to teethe and he knew his time had come.

All was well, the fates had balanced, and he could see his Naomi walking into their bedroom. He stood up and crossed over to meet her.

"You're finally ready, are you?" she commented to him in that teasing wifely manner he had always adored. "You're worse than an old woman you realize? Meddling all the time," she groused.

Zachariah laughed and held up his hands in mock surrender.

"Come on, Naomi. You know I had to make it right. Besides, it has been you these last few years kicking my ass to keep on going. You know little Janine Simmonds had always had that childish crush on me. She never believed I was way too old for her. I felt awful over all her problems. I considered her practically family. Anyway, it's all turned out well. Roland and Helene have their children and health and, now that Edward and Christiana are so happy together, we can finally go on that adventure you were always promising me, hmm?"

Naomi Rutledge came forward and pulled her True Mate and soul-love close. They hugged companionably. Then she leaned closer, and lifted her head. Zachariah lowered his head and kissed her passionately.

"Mmmm," he murmured against her lips, "I've missed this. Let's start that adventure. I'm ready now."

Without even letting his True Mate answer, he went back to kissing her, sliding his tongue erotically inside her mouth, just the way he knew she loved.

Leading her over to the bed, he gently lowered her there, and promptly lost himself in her body.

* * * * *

Feeling something strange in the house, Artemais climbed up to the Old Man's room to ask if he could scent it as well. Artemais admitted to himself he also had this burning need to see the Old Man. He had been acting strangely all day and secretly Artemais was a bit worried.

He was saddened, but not shocked, to find the Old Man lying on the bed, fully clothed. He had his eyes shut with a huge grin on his face. Artemais bent over him, planning on covering him with a comforter.

Until he realized his chest neither rose nor fell. Suddenly, he knew what or, more accurately, who the strange presence was. He sat back on the chair, feeling happy and incredibly sad at the same time.

"Take care of him, Grandma," he said, feeling foolish, but remarkably right at the same time. "Gramps has been hanging around a bit too long. I'm glad he finally let you come and take him back. May we all be so blessed at the end."

Outside, Artemais heard his new grandbaby laughing and shrieking. Smiling sadly, he headed back out to his family.

TWIN TEMPTATIONS

Chapter One

೫

The ballroom was packed with assorted Rutledge extended family, friends and coworkers. The formal benefit for the wolf foundation had brought everyone out in their most dressy, exquisite outfits, and as usual people were having a blast, laughing, dancing and drinking the night away. Samantha Monique Rutledge, however, stood silently in a corner of the room and tried not to fidget in her elegant dark green cocktail dress as she smiled and waved to the people who passed her by. Sipping at the flute of champagne in hand, Samantha debated the wisdom of trying to cross over to the buffet table in her stiletto heels. Werewolf power and strength didn't come in the least bit useful when it came to balancing in needle-thin high heels.

"Sammi!"

Samantha grinned and waved as her twin brother, Alexander, headed toward her, his hand firmly clasped in his long-time girlfriend, Isabel's. An unknown but dashingly handsome tall, blond man kept pace with the couple, and the three of them crossed to where she stood.

"Al, darling." Samantha laughed at the exuberance her twin exhibited. "Better lay off that champagne, or Bella will need to drive you home."

Alexander waved her comment aside with ease. The twins had always been exceptionally close, and growing into adults with their own lives had not changed the love and deep bond they had always shared. Although mind reading was not common between werewolves, Samantha and Alexander had always been able to communicate privately between themselves, deepening their link. Teasing between them was par for the course, and they both knew that where and when it counted, they were there for each other like almost no one else could ever be.

"You should be out there dancing and partying, Sammi," Alex chided her seriously. "This is supposed to be a celebration. Luckily for you, I found you a dance partner."

Samantha raised an eyebrow as Alex waved at the stranger. She didn't get the chance to interject, however, as Alex ploughed on before she could catch her breath.

"Sammi, this is Bella's cousin, Callum MacLennon. Callum, this is my twin sister, Samantha Rutledge."

Sam could feel her face flush in embarrassment. Ever since Alexander had fallen so hopelessly in love with Bella, he had been determined that she be as blissfully happy as he. He didn't seem to understand that she already felt perfectly happy with her freedom and single status.

On the other hand, she wasn't about to turn down a bit of dancing from a sexy man either. His blond hair was neatly slicked into the popular "just out of bed" casual messy look, and his dark green eyes—very similar eyes to his cousin, Bella—sparkled with laughter, interest and that slightly awkward "we're being set up" look, which Samantha felt sure was currently reflected in her own dark blue eyes.

Samantha assumed this not-so-subtle setup of her brother's had come as a bit of a surprise to Callum as well as herself. Despite the small uncertainty she could see in his eyes, he gallantly held out his hand to lead her to the dance floor, curiosity etched onto his face as they surveyed each other casually. Smiling, knowing one dance couldn't possibly hurt anything except her feet in these damn stilettos, Samantha took Callum's offered hand with a warm, genuine smile.

"My cousin and your brother have painfully little tact when it comes to their Cupid skills, don't you think?" Callum chuckled as he led her onto the packed dance floor. "I thought since I'm leaving next week for Australia, Bella might have actually laid off my case for once." Samantha smiled in sympathy and shrugged her shoulder. Resting one hand gently on her partner's upper arm, Samantha shivered at the slight tingle that ran through her body as Callum wove their fingers together and they slowly began to move to the slow music.

"Alex has only become really bad since falling like a ton of bricks for Bella," Sam said, defending her twin. "And Bella mentioned your project work with dingoes. It sounds really interesting."

Callum and Samantha smiled at each other and continued to dance. "Actually, I was plotting my own escape," she confessed with a wicked chuckle. "I have a mountain of work I really should be doing, and it's fizzled any party mood I had worked up."

Samantha grinned impishly at Callum's raised eyebrow and looked deviously over her shoulder to where Alex and Bella now hovered at the edge of the dance floor swaying slightly, their bodies melded together. She could easily tell the couple was engrossed only in each other, and so she should be fine to make her escape soon.

"Will you help me break out of here?" she asked, laughter in her tone. Samantha began to lead them both, still dancing, toward the back exit. She was only teasing Callum, had no intention of him playing Sir Knight, so his response came as somewhat of a surprise.

"Now how can I resist such a request?" he chuckled, and took over the lead. Dancing their way carefully to the opposite edge of the floor, and then working their way cautiously through the crowd, Samantha had trouble stifling her laughter. Callum had taken on the air of someone attempting to be stealthy and happily failing miserably.

Giggling as they reached the back door, Samantha cast one last quick glance over her shoulder, pleased that she could no longer see either her parents or her brother, and ducked outside into the cool evening air.

"That's priceless," she laughed. "Thank you so much! For the laugh as well as the escape."

Impulsively, Samantha wrapped her arms around Callum's neck and kissed him softly and swiftly on the lips. It was a chaste kiss, but it sent a shudder of heat and need exploding through her body. Samantha pulled back, a slightly startled look on her face, as the heat and intensity of her reaction had caught her completely by surprise.

"Uh..." she stuttered as she blinked her eyes and wondered how a mere kiss could effectively change her from being an impish vixen into a blithering idiot in under five seconds.

Callum cupped her jaw in one strong, tanned hand and drew her mouth back to his. Their lips met a second time, and the world seemed to slow down to a complete stop. Callum easily slid his tongue inside her parted lips, and they tasted each other, both of them eating at each other's lips and mouths. Callum pulled her closer, and Samantha could feel the heat of his body press against hers. When one of his powerful thighs slid between her legs, she could feel the thick hardness of his erection press against her lower belly and aching pussy.

Panting now, Samantha arched herself into Callum's warmth, her body wanting nothing more than to rub against him, her legs already spreading, her pussy damp and craving his thick shaft to plunge inside her. Her cheeks flushed with arousal, Samantha turned her head to the side as Callum began to string nipping kissing down her neck.

The thin, silky material of her gown rasped as Callum's pelvis and thigh rubbed against her body, the friction heightening her arousal. Samantha shivered as Callum's lips and teeth teased her, his warm hands moving down from her jaw to clasp her shoulder and tug her closer towards his own overheated body. Without thinking, Samantha lifted a leg to wrap around Callum's hips. This brought her pussy directly over his hard cock, straining against the zipper of his slacks, and as she rubbed, the soft rustle of silk against linen had them both moaning again.

Samantha laid her hand over Callum's on her ass and led him up and under the short hem of her dress, guiding his hand toward her naked pussy. She swallowed his gasp as his fingers touched the soft, short hair barely covering her, and without any further invitation his fingers dipped inside her to become slick with her cream. The tip of his index finger stroked out to caress her hard clit, and Samantha let her head fall back in ecstasy as she moaned deeply.

"No panties?" Callum gasped, excitement and eagerness dripping from his tone. Samantha grinned wickedly and cupped his face in her hands. She watched his pupils dilate, making the green in his eyes deepen at his heightening need as she kissed him slowly, licked his lips and nibbled lightly on his full lower lip.

"Even a thong showed a line through the thinness of this dress material," she said huskily, "and so it was easier to go without."

Callum rocked into her body, his erection again pressing hard and insistently into her barely covered pussy. She was wet, ready for him and more than eager. Samantha had never responded this quickly to someone or been this needy after hardly five minutes acquaintance, but for now, she knew all she needed to know. A hard, sexy, totally fuckable good man.

"I need to know you're with me here, Sam," Callum groaned, his restraint obviously coming close to its end. Samantha chuckled wickedly and tightened her leg around his waist, rocking herself against his cock and pressing her breasts into his chest. Her erect, tight nipples rubbed against the silky material of her dress and caused a spasm of delight to course from nipple to clit.

"The back door is supposed to be the fire exit," she panted. "No one is supposed to use it. I promise I'm with you here, Callum, so please, fuck me right here against the wall."

"There's a condom in my wallet," Callum groaned as he pushed her hard, but not roughly, against the wall beside the door. Samantha's hand dived into Callum's pocket almost before he had finished his sentence and withdrew his wallet, finding the small foil wrapper with ease.

She dropped the wallet, but thankfully not the condom, as a warm, large hand worked its way down the front of her dress and cupped her breast, a wickedly skilful thumb sliding over her nipple and tweaking it expertly.

"Fuck, yes," she panted, her back automatically arching up into the erotic caress. Her hands fumbled slightly as she unzipped Callum's pants and pushed soft, cotton boxer briefs down to free the large cock that strained his pants.

They exchanged hot, biting kisses as Callum continued to play with her breasts, and Samantha ripped the foil package open and hurriedly eased the thin latex down to cover the massive cock. His pre-cum lubricated the condom and heat pulsated through the plastic from his engorged dick. Callum spread the skirt of her dress back so he could open her legs and let his fingers roam her pussy better.

"Don't want to hurt you," he murmured softly as he slicked his fingers in her juices and coated his cock. Samantha chuckled softly, cupped his face and brought him close to her so she could kiss him tenderly.

"I am so ready," she insisted softly. "It's been a while and I haven't reacted like this in…in ages."

Samantha had been about to admit she had *never* felt like this before, but stopped herself from stating it. Instead she opened herself wider and drew Callum's hips closer until they were pressed tightly against each other and his cock was nestled at her entrance.

"Please Callum," she said huskily, her eyes steadily holding his so he could see she was serious and not teasing. "Fuck me. Fuck me right now. I want you inside me."

Callum groaned, and she gasped as in one swift, hard movement he sheathed himself deeply inside her, his thickness and length taking Samantha slightly by surprise. It really *had* been a while since she had indulged in sex, work and her small PI business keeping her exceedingly busy. And it had been a *very* long time since she'd had sex that meant anything other than a quick, passing fuck. Somehow, with Callum right now, this seemed to her as more than just a quick fuck-against-the-wall fling.

Filled until her body was stretched, Samantha panted and clung to Callum, her short nails digging into his arm and hip, leaving small marks behind in his flesh.

"Fuck." He panted hard, holding himself still while her body adjusted to his size and width. "You are so fucking tight. You're amazing."

"You're pretty damn good yourself," Samantha chuckled as she caught her breath, squirming against the hard wall so she could rock her hips slightly and press him even further inside her. "Please don't stop, Callum. I'm so fucking hot and you're so thick, this isn't going to last long."

Samantha gasped as Callum bent his head to lick her neck, and then bite into it. His teeth stung, but didn't break her flesh, and it was the most potently erotic and dominant thing any man had ever done to her. It heated her blood to volcanic levels, and Samantha felt her body jump into overdrive.

No man had ever really dominated her. It was particularly hard since as a werewolf she was so very much more powerful physically than any human man. She didn't like pain or most bondage games, and so she never sought such men as her sporadic lovers. As such, she had never had a man truly bite her or mark her, never felt that thrill of being completely and fully possessed, branded. Feeling just a small measure of it now, here with Callum, made her even more weak at the knees.

"Callum," she panted, unable to even articulate anything further. Callum withdrew from her body, causing her to cry out in denial, but he quickly thrust back into her, hard enough to press her body back into the wall.

Samantha bit gently back into the soft juncture between Callum's neck and shoulder as he thrust inside her. Her pussy tightened around his thrusting cock, clinging onto him as if he were a lifeline. Callum pressed her hips back with one large hand, the change in angle helping him rub over her G-spot. Her body tightened, began to convulse, and Samantha cried out.

"You're beautiful," Callum panted as he licked over the small, slightly bruised area of skin on her neck. "I want to watch your face and eyes as you come for me, as you scream my name."

Samantha watched as Callum pulled back, his lips full and begging to be kissed, his eyes dark and sparkling with lust and hunger. She smiled at him, reached a hand out to twist in his blond hair. She was about to tease him, but his thick length stroked over her G-spot again, and she knew her climax would come soon.

"Come with me," she whimpered, almost pleaded. Her mind spun dizzyingly, but all Samantha knew was this time she wanted Callum to be there on the brink of climax and fall over, let himself go with her as she came. Callum grunted at the extra sensation, and his thrusts grew harder, rougher, and her back was pressed into the wall until the pleasure of his strokes began to make the uncomfortable friction add to the exquisite sensations rocking her body.

"I want to taste your clit," Callum said softly, his voice rough and husky with the strain of holding his own climax back. "I want to feel your climax on my tongue. I bet you taste hot and spicy, like honey, only better."

Samantha whimpered, and when Callum's finger stroked over her clit again, her world exploded. The mental image of Callum eating her out, his hot tongue stroking over her clit as he tasted her climax pushed her over the edge, and her body shook with the force of her orgasm. The tight contractions of her pussy milked Callum's cock and he cried out, thrusting into her even harder than before as he rode through his own climax.

Warmth enfolded her as Callum gathered her in his arms and held her against the brick wall. It took a moment for Sam to realize she had just let herself be fucked against the side of the building. Even in the middle of the night people still walked the streets, and although they were mostly shielded from view around the back, a thrill of delicious naughtiness ran through her at the thought of how very easily they could have been caught.

Slowly, Samantha kissed Callum, nipping lightly on his full lower lip, exchanging slow licks with her tongue and tasting him lazily.

"Mmmm," she murmured softly as their hands slowly traced the outlines of each other's body. The urgent heat and rush had passed now, and they were able to take their time. After a moment Callum withdrew from her body, picked up his dropped wallet and pulled his handkerchief out of his pocket. Quickly, he disposed of the condom. Samantha shivered slightly in the cool night breeze as she rearranged her dress.

As Samantha watched Callum crumple the handkerchief and tuck it away, she really looked at him. At just over six feet, with his mussed blond hair and hard, muscled body he could easily have been a model for any sexy women's magazine. And those smoldering green eyes just made her knees weak.

Thrills of heat ran through her body, even though her arms were bare in the cool evening. Samantha blinked as something Alex had said came back to her.

When I first met Bella, I almost thought I'd contracted a fever, I was just so warm, so hungry and desperate for her. Don't look at me like that, Sammi, you'll understand one day. I just craved her, could stare at her for hours on end and never grow bored. It was instant true love, I tell you.

A small kernel of panic formed in her chest. She didn't have time to fall in love. Her business was tiny and she was working long, hard days. While having children and settling down were definitely in her long term plans, at only twenty-eight, Sam had always assumed she would get around to that "later". Now just simply wasn't the time.

Calm down, Callum is leaving for a whole other continent. There is no need for getting ahead of yourself here.

Samantha smiled and chastely kissed Callum's cheek as he returned to her, his own clothes wrinkled, but back in place.

"I really do need to get moving," she said with genuine apology. A part of her wanted to stay here and beg Callum to follow her home. Her large bed beckoned, wicked fantasies of handcuffs and heating oil, of hearing this large man whimper and beg and plead for her to suck him, to touch him, to make him come, all bouncing around in her head. Samantha had never been particularly serious about any of her lovers, though until starting her own business had swamped her personal time, she had enjoyed indulging in regular flings.

Pushing away the knowledge that this was different, that something about this man touched her very deeply and maybe even irrevocably, Samantha insisted to herself she was just letting her imagination run away from her.

This time with Callum, for some inexplicable reason, had been the first sex she had allowed herself to really let go and just be herself. Samantha had unleashed a small part of her more animalistic side, and it had given her such satisfaction, such an air of satiation that it was meddling with her brain.

For a split second, Samantha thought she saw hurt flash across Callum's eyes, but it was gone before she could be certain. She opened her mouth, searching for the right words to say, but Callum smiled and kissed her warmly, gave her a small half-hug.

"Always happy to help a woman in need," he said casually. His hand reached out, his fingers lightly tracing the line of her jaw in contrast to the studied ease of his words, and

Samantha almost changed her mind. Callum moved away, however, and together they began to walk out toward the main street.

"Bella or Alexander would have mentioned I leave for Australia. I landed a job with the Dingo Conservation Project over there. It's the job of a lifetime."

Samantha smiled and nodded, paused for a moment as Callum halted at a big black truck and fished his keys out.

"Need a lift?" he asked.

Samantha considered it for a moment. Callum had put no extra weight on the words—he truly appeared to be simply offering her a lift, but she didn't trust herself not to drag him back into her apartment and give them both a second helping of delicious sex. She hungered to lick and suck him all over, to insist he lick and suck *her* as he had so blatantly suggested earlier.

And so she shook her head. "No, but thanks. My apartment block is not very far up the road."

Large, warm hands circled her waist and drew her between his spread legs. Callum leaned against the side of his truck and they kissed hungrily, passionately. Samantha sucked on his tongue and reveled in the moan she elicited. They were both flushed and panting as he let her go and she pulled away, and only a fool could have missed the once again thick, hot erection pressing against his slacks.

"I'm not sure this is over," Callum said softly, almost as if he were musing to himself. Samantha smiled slightly sadly, but couldn't deny the situation felt incomplete to her as well. Instead of commenting or acknowledging, however, she simply nodded.

"Be safe in Australia," she said gently, honestly meaning the words. Forcing herself to not linger, she turned and walked down the road toward her home. When she licked her lips, she could still taste the masculine, spicy flavor that she knew was Callum's alone, and she would never be able to forget it.

Chapter Two
Eight months later…

ॐ

"Come on, Sammi…Dammit, you know you owe me."

"Excuse me?" Samantha exclaimed in astonishment, tempted to stare at the phone in her hand as if she could actually glimpse her twin through the handset. "*I* owe *you*? Since when, darling brother? It was I who helped you the last time. *You* owe *me*, according to my count."

Samantha walked around her apartment as she enjoyed the banter. She knew full well it didn't matter what Alexander wanted her help with, she would drop everything and rush to him if needed. It simply spoiled all the fun of their teasing if she caved in an instantly said yes to any old request he made.

Their close bond helped her know without doubt that while Alexander did need her help this time, it was not something super urgent. To make matters confusing, though, she could also feel him keeping something back from her — so she felt no guilt whatsoever in teasing him.

"Come on, Al, spill. I appreciate the call, truly, but I know you're up to something. So what is it?"

"Me? Up to something? Sammi, I am hurt!"

Samantha smiled. "Al, dearest, you only ever call me Sammi when you are either sick, worried or want something, and you know it. So talk. What favor do you need and why are you wheedling me?"

"Fine. I need your help." Alexander sighed heavily and almost dramatically on the other end of the phone line. "Happy now?"

Samantha did laugh at this.

"Oh, please! Explain. You know I'll help you, but you have to *tell* me what I am doing and why first. Then we can negotiate the terms."

"I can't tell you all of it," Alexander started, and Samantha found herself frowning.

Firstly, Alex hadn't risen to the bait of their negotiations, which was almost unheard of between them. Since she had guessed Alexander was holding back and knew it was unusual for him to not tell her everything, Samantha could smell something going on.

Samantha felt a moment of panic, "It's not Bella, is it. Is she okay? What's happened?"

"No, no. Bella is fine. I need you to help investigate those two wolf cubs that went missing last week. I also want you to look into the employee who's just been promoted to run the Wolf Reintroduction Program. The problem is I need you to be utterly discreet about it all. The man is Callum MacLennon."

Samantha felt her stomach tighten. Alexander's secrecy and hesitancy suddenly made a hell of a lot of sense. Alexander didn't know she and Callum had fucked each other blind that night—or if he did, he hadn't let on he knew. Neither could her brother possibly known that she had buried herself in her work to try to keep tempting and wicked fantasies about the handsome blond out of her mind.

Samantha knew her brother's hesitancy would be more because Bella adored her cousin, and if Alex expressed even faint distrust in the man it would cause all kinds of grief between him and his True Mate. Problem was, spending any amount of time in close quarters with Callum could be hazardous to *her* own way of life right now.

"Callum?" she stammered. "But...but Bella will kill me! Not to mention castrate you and cut your heart into millions of tiny pieces."

"You think I don't know this, Sammi? But there have been some strange goings on under his watch. Two of the cubs we tried to bring in safely were lost in transit. I think we have a leak, and Callum solely is in charge of those cubs. I could really use your help, as well as your nose for digging out the truth behind the story."

"Really?" Samantha tried desperately to stall while she forced her brain into action. "I thought he was working down in Australia with dingoes. When did he come back?"

"Two weeks ago. His work with the dingoes was excellent. So when he moved back to America, Bella and I decided to let him help with the fieldwork side of the foundation. Look, how about you just come to the annual dinner? Reacquaint yourself with him, chat and try to catch up with him. You can visit the office one day soon and look into his work, talk to him and find out what's really been happening.

"You wouldn't even need to lie about your ties to the Foundation really, you do sometimes write up articles for us, and you're the only person I trust to be careful and quiet about this. Like you said, Bella will kill me if she thinks I'm having him investigated. Can you help me? Please, Sammi?"

Samantha took a deep breath. Her brother was obviously neck-deep in this problem, and with his abiding love for Bella clouding his judgment, he really couldn't step back and investigate this himself.

Why the hell not investigate Callum MacLennon? Samantha found it hard to believe the man she had been intimate with could harm innocent little wolf cubs, but then she had been in Callum's presence for all of half an hour. One of the few things she had learned in her digging the truth out was just how easy it was for people to show only one side of themselves.

Most people only saw what they wished to see, not what was actually staring at them in the face. Loath as she was to admit it, Alexander's wanting more details was sensible, and she was in a good position to search the answers he needed.

"Okay then, Alex," Samantha agreed, wrinkling her nose against the windowpane. "Fax me any details you can, along with a copy of the operation Callum was supposed to do. I'll look into it from my end and see you tomorrow night at the annual dinner. This isn't some lame scheme to make sure I do turn up to the damn dinner, is it?"

"Of course not," Alex chuckled, sounding for the first time like his usual self once again. Samantha had to smile as his relief crashed over her. At least she knew without a doubt he was genuinely relieved and pleased she had taken the job. "But I would like to politely request you wear the red dress, Sammi. It really complements your hair and eyes."

Samantha smiled, knowing Alexander would be able to feel her amusement as easily as she felt his relief.

"Go shove yourself, brother dear. If you like the red so much, *you* wear it." As soon as the words left her mouth she knew what his response would be and she laughed, before he could even say it. "I know, you simply don't have the figure for that dress, but you know exactly what I mean. Why don't you wear that red tie with little horned devils on it that Bella bought you for Christmas?"

"I wouldn't want to upstage you, my dear."

Samantha laughed and closed her eyes, enjoyed the feel of the sun on her face. "Okay, I'll wear the red, but only for you, darling twin. Only for you."

They said their goodbyes and she hung up the phone. Samantha silently repeated in her mind how it was only for Alexander that she had agreed to look into Callum MacLennon.

Samantha had been depressingly celibate since her encounter with Callum. She had found she didn't want anyone else's hands running over her skin. She didn't want the feel of another man palming her breasts or rubbing her clit or stroking deeply inside her. It was Callum's hands she wanted caressing her, doing those unspeakably intimate things with her, *to* her.

No man had ever made her knees so weak, had made her body fill with a craving, desperate yearning like this.

Samantha crossed back over from the window and firmly forced herself to focus on her work. Pacing over to her desk and picking up a new notebook and pen, Samantha sat down cross-legged on the couch and began to make notes. She made a list of the things she wanted to check into before going to the annual dinner for the wolf foundation. The fax hummed softly as Alexander sent through the report she needed to go over, and she added a note to that effect to her list.

Standing up, she crossed to the small machine and began pulling pages out of the tray as they came through. Glad to feel her mind busily ticking away once more, she set to work.

Chapter Three

🔊

Callum MacLennon internally winced in sympathy as he watched his cousin glide up to him on three-inch stiletto heels that sparkled almost as much as her shimmering, slinky silver gown. She had a radiant smile on her face and her green eyes — almost identical to his own — were sparkling brightly.

Nothing, however, could detract attention away from the heart-shaped diamond set in platinum on her finger, with two star-shaped emeralds cuddling close. Callum felt his heart simultaneously constrict and lift.

Only a fool would think it was anything other than an engagement ring, and while he was quite honestly ecstatic that his very best friend had found happiness, it only made his own loneliness seem all the greater. Callum knew without even needing to ask that she was the happiest woman on Earth, and for that he smiled as he warmly embraced Bella in greeting.

"I hear congratulations are in order, Bella. You could have told me yourself, you know."

"I'm sorry, Cal. I meant to call you first thing this morning when we finally managed to get out of bed, but everything has just been such a whirl. I take it Will or Josephine told you?"

Callum stepped back, reluctantly ending the embrace and shook his head.

"Nah, with half the Rutledge clan here I heard it from one of the kids at the front door. He recognized me and was practically gushing. I think it was Julien, Alexander's next sibling, but it could have been Theo. I've only met half these people a time or two, so it's rather hard to tell some of them apart."

Bella waved a hand airily. "You'll be seeing lots more of everyone now that you're back permanently. I'm sorry you didn't hear it from me first. This is the first chance I've had to speak to you—I got so caught up in everything during the day. I know you've been busy and upset over those cubs, so I figured you could use the good news."

Callum could practically feel the evening begin to dim.

"I still don't have many leads at all on them, Bella. Either there's been a hell of a lot of money to grease the wheels or this was one seriously organized affair. But I *will* find those cubs and get them back."

He bent forward slightly as Bella stood on tiptoes to kiss his cheek softly and give him another quick hug.

"I know you will, Cal. But Alexander has hired someone to help you."

Callum stiffened. He tried really, *really* hard not to feel outraged. He liked and respected Alexander Rutledge, knew Bella loved him more than anything, and so he really didn't want to upset his cousin.

"Alex can go fuck himself." Callum barely managed to keep the heat of anger from his tone. Even so, Bella raised an eyebrow at his language. "Look, I know it was my oversight that caused those tiny cubs to get stolen. If I had been guarding them myself and traveling with them instead of packing myself up to move here then we wouldn't have needed to hire those idiots—"

He halted his tirade when Bella placed a finger over his lips. He smiled wryly, knowing she felt just as bad, just as worried as he did.

"This isn't meant as a punishment, Cal. Alex contacted his twin, Samantha. She's a private investigator, and a damn fine one too. She's just going to help you look into everything, be a second set of eyes for you. Now I know you don't want help…"

Callum felt himself fairly bristling with the insinuation he couldn't deal with the situation. He knew Alexander didn't think him incompetent, or if he did he certainly wouldn't say so aloud as Bella would tear his heart out, werewolf or not, yet he couldn't help how he felt and reacted to the news.

"It's not that I don't just *want* any help in this, Bella. I don't *need* any help. I know Samantha is a PI, but this was my mistake, my problem. The last thing I need is another Rutledge hovering over my every move and taking tales back to Brother Dearest."

Callum resisted the urge to smile as Bella's eyes flashed in anger.

"Samantha *won't* be telling on you or anyone else, and don't you dare insult her like that. I love you to death, Cal, you *know* that, but Sam is a good friend of mine. She can help you. You're not the he-man you seem to think you are.

"I have every faith that you will do your job and do it brilliantly, but tracking down those cubs is something Sam can definitely help you with, and I don't want your stupid masculine pride getting in the way. Am I clear?"

Callum laughed softly and shook his head. One thing he had to credit Alexander Rutledge with, he had brought his shy little cousin out of her shell and helped her become the incredible woman he had always known she was.

"So what *exactly* are you saying here, Bella? Level with me."

For a moment, he caught a flicker of...something...in his cousin's eyes. He had no idea what the fleeting emotion was, but his instincts flared to life. There was more going on here than he knew about.

"I want you to work with Sam, Callum. No stonewalling, no idiotic male posturing. Sam is going to be working with you and I want you to help her and stick close to her."

Callum felt his eyes slit half-closed. Usually he could scent a lie a mile away, and Bella had never been the best of liars. He warily eyed at his cousin.

Something was most definitely up, and for the first time in years he had no idea what it was and couldn't read his cousin properly. She was deliberately not meeting his eyes and being very careful with her body language.

"Stick close with Samantha Rutledge? Work with her? That's not a problem, Bella. I can play nicely when told to. What else aren't you telling me?"

When Bella nibbled nervously on her lower lip he *knew* she was up to something. A million thoughts ran through his head, all of them more ridiculous than the next.

He had never told his cousin about the most memorable fuck of his life—partly because he believed if Samantha wanted Bella to know about their sexual interlude she'd tell her herself, but also because a part of him still felt astonished he had been unable to control himself and taken her against the wall in a dark alleyway. Neither was he keen to admit to Bella that he had been half in love with Samantha ever since that fateful evening. Callum was used to dealing with his life himself. He didn't want or need Bella to run interference for him.

Working with Samantha would be a pleasure. Maybe he could even work her out of his system if the opportunity presented itself correctly. If Bella was hiding something. though...

Before he could start questioning Bella more closely, Alexander had snuck up behind her and embraced her, pressing kisses to her neck. Callum winced and averted his face.

"Please, Alex, some of us want to be able to stomach these expensive canapés, not watch you make a scene."

"Come on, Cal, I would have thought a man like you could stand to watch a few kisses."

Callum shrugged and cast his eye over the crowded ballroom. When he caught sight of a particular brunette in a stunning red dress, he felt his breath hitch. When she turned slightly to look at him, he felt his heart accelerate, beating hard against his chest.

Samantha.

She was, if possible, even more beautiful than she had been eight months ago. He felt his cock harden, making him shift subtly in his tuxedo pants. The last thing he wanted or needed was for Alexander to notice him stiffen and all but pant after his twin sister.

Callum snagged a glass of champagne from a passing waiter and turned back to Bella.

"Play nice, huh?" he said cryptically, desperately wanting to inquire deeper into his cousin's *real* reasons behind her little speech. Alex could just have easily told him he had hired Samantha to help him look into the cubs' disappearance, yet it had been Bella who had taken him aside.

When Bella merely nodded and leaned back into Alex's embrace, Callum shook his head. He stalked away to the nearest plate of funny-looking canapés. Eyeing them carefully, not wanting to eat goose liver or something equally distasteful, he finally speared a cheese and pickle concoction and popped it into his mouth.

"It's been a while, Callum. I thought you were in Australia working with dingoes."

Callum turned around and swallowed hard, barely managing not to choke himself.

Samantha Rutledge was one gorgeous woman, all luscious curves encased just so in a perfect slinky red dress. It technically revealed little skin other than her arms and a small amount of back, but the way it clung to her breasts and whispered between her thighs with her every movement, a man couldn't help but be able to visualize every inch of her delectable skin.

141

"Project finished, Sammi. I figured it was time to come home." Callum drawled in his most jaded, arrogantly cynical tone as he tried to hide some of the lust spearing through him and heating his blood until he could swear he was about to explode.

The woman looked like a living, walking, talking wet dream.

His personal, private and exceedingly lifelike wet dream.

She opened her mouth, and once again his instincts kicked into gear. She was about to tell him off for using her familiar, childhood family name. He decided to switch gears. Seduction could come after he found out if she was in on Bella's crazy scheme, whatever the hell it was.

"I've been warned to play nicely with you, Sam. Do you think we can learn to play well together?"

The very faint flush that crept across her cheeks had his cock hardening even more. Yet he also saw curiosity and an uncertainty in her eyes. She was wary of him, rightly so since the only thing his mind seemed focused on was ripping the slinky red dress from her body, spreading her open on the nearest available flat surface and finally being able to take his time in exploring the luscious curves of her body.

Callum had spent eight months fantasizing about her body, the way she whimpered when he penetrated her and how mewling little cries escaped her mouth when she was about to come. Nothing could give him greater pleasure than finally being able to take his time with her, to look, see, touch and taste every inch of her, and he wasn't sure he could focus a hundred percent on anything else until he had satisfied himself with her.

Samantha's eyes burned with lustful curiosity, but no deceit or hidden agenda lay in those dark blue depths. What he could see were her peaked nipples rasping against the slinky red material of her dress. He felt his cock lengthen and tighten even more. He knew no amount of painful shifting would hide the iron rod lodged behind the fly of his tux.

Might as well wear it with pride, he decided.

Besides, her innocence in Bella's plan, whatever it might be, was well worth the side benefits of *having* to stick close to her.

"I think we need to talk," he rasped, surprised at the scratchiness in his throat. A moment of staring at this woman and he wanted to do a million wicked things to her, in front of most of her family, her parents and a quarter of the foundation's rich, snobby donors.

He must be insane.

Callum gently grabbed Samantha's arm, turned her so they exited the side doors and led them into the dark gardens. She laughed, the happy sound floating around him and only making him want to hear if she would laugh differently in the throes of passion. "No one has ever accused you of being shy or hesitant, have they, Callum?"

He smiled, "Not a chance, baby. I am known for my directness."

"I'm beginning to believe it," she replied, looking at him and making his mind all fuzzy.

Every thought except for kissing her senseless flew from his mind. As he led her outside, they walked in step. He knew no matter what that he would enjoy working with this wonderfully sassy, beautiful woman.

Chapter Four

ℒ

Samantha smiled in the darkness as the sounds of the gala dinner grew dimmer and dimmer. She hadn't bothered to fight Callum when he had insisted on this walk. They needed to talk and she didn't want to spoil the dinner for herself by having to think too much about what needed to be said.

Her mind wanted to do one thing, her body another. And while this impressive debate raged within herself, she also tried to keep uppermost in mind that she was supposed to be asking intelligent questions about the two lost cubs and trying to find if Callum had had anything to do with it.

And so, in the split second she had been given to decide whether or not to "follow" Callum out here, she had decided to spend a few minutes privately out here in the darkness of the garden, the scent of the earth, wind and trees around her, rather than spend half the night stewing in her own doubts and questions.

When the music from the ballroom was just a faint sound, barely heard, and the night wind whispered softly between them both, both she and Callum halted beneath the leafy branches of a tree.

"You should be arrested for wearing such a dress," he said softly, roughly. Samantha laughed.

"Not even my *father* could get me for public indecency in this dress. Besides, it's positively chaste and Victorian compared to what some of our guests are wearing."

"Those Victorians were a rather sexually enlightened group, Sammi, darling." Callum replied with a wicked grin and an evil twinkle in his eye. "Besides, I don't feel the overwhelming urge to strip anyone else I've seen tonight, baby. Only you."

Samantha shivered as he said her name with such an intimate familiarity. A part of her felt like they had just made shattering love and were lying next to each other in bed, sharing a pillow and whispering soft words to each other.

She pulled herself from the hazy fantasy. She needed to keep her mind on real, legitimate matters, not indulge in dreams, she reminded herself sternly.

"Tomorrow I will be coming into the office," she started, not letting Callum even get a word in to argue. "Mostly to look over the records and anything you might have on the cubs. Is that okay?" she finished, more for politeness' sake than as an actual request.

She watched as Callum literally shook himself and cleared his throat. When he spoke, his voice was still deep, but sounded practically normal once again.

"Sure. I have a few leads I'm chasing, but nothing much. A fresh set of eyes might be exactly what's needed."

She smiled, knowing he couldn't see her clearly in the dark. Clenching her hand into a fist, resisting the temptation to reach out and stroke his jaw, or worse, rest her head against his chest and listen to his heartbeat.

Plenty of times she had been to social affairs with men in tuxes, but none of them looked as handsome or debonair as Callum.

Samantha averted her face and drew in a deep breath of fresh air, but she could still scent him. His scent had not changed in the months they had been apart, he was still musky, darkly masculine and smelled of wood and the wild. Knowing it was a mistake, and at this single moment not caring, she turned her face toward him again and stepped forward to close the distance between them. She wrapped her arm around his waist and drew him in to her. Lifting her head slightly she took her time kissing his lips.

Light and color exploded around her, rocked her world. She had been right, he did still taste hot and spicy and so delicious that she could barely cope with it. He quickly took over the kiss. She felt his hand splay over her back, draw her up into the heat of his body as his mouth opened to plunder her own.

Callum's tongue slid into her mouth, teasing and playing erotically with hers. They tangled, hands seeking skin underneath clothing, both breathing deeply as the fire of their kiss raged out of control.

Samantha had never felt like this, not with any of her previous lovers, casual or not.

As she tasted him, reveled in the spicy, masculine taste invading her senses, she breathed deeply of his scent and felt her heart momentarily stop, and then pound furiously fast.

He is definitely your One, her mind screamed at her. *Mate with him! Mark him as yours so no other woman can get to him!*

She didn't need a True Mate, didn't *want* to give the potential for devastation and heartbreak to anyone just yet. But at the same time, she couldn't deny the attraction and potent reaction she had to Callum.

"We really shouldn't..." Samantha pulled away, but Callum put a finger to her mouth before she could finish the sentence. Callum didn't move his hand from her back, continued to hold her close, and she breathed his scent in one last time before wrenching herself from his arms.

"Why exactly shouldn't we be doing this, Sammi? I have no other commitments, and there is no way you can convince me you didn't enjoy that kiss."

Samantha felt her stomach flop, but ruthlessly kept herself under control.

"We're going to be working together," she started, mentally slapping herself. She was supposed to be seeing if he had anything to do with the disappearance of the cubs! Not to mention keeping an eye on his investigation. Samantha embraced her anger with herself. If she could keep angry and ignore the aching need within her, everything would be much easier and she would do a better job for her twin.

"I don't see why we can't work together on the case and not spend time out of work hours together, Sam," Callum said patiently, with a dogged persistence Sam couldn't help but admire. "What aren't you telling me, darling?" he asked suspiciously, causing her heart to accelerate.

Damn him for being savvy to her!

Samantha turned around and headed back toward the ballroom with long strides.

"Sam!" She shivered as she felt Callum call out and grab her arm again. Thankfully, he didn't try to stop her, only held her gently as they walked back to the dinner party together.

"Fine, don't tell me what's going on right now," he conceded, "but at least admit to me how you enjoyed the kiss."

Samantha bit her lip and looked at Callum.

In the better light, she could only stare at the handsomeness of his face. His blond hair was mussed, and she remembered the soft, silky feel of it in her hands just moments earlier.

"Fine," she said softly, disgusted with her inability to lie to him. "I enjoyed the kiss, but that doesn't make it right. I don't fuck people that I work with. Besides, personally I think finding those two lost cubs is far more important than us rolling around ripping up the sheets, don't you?"

She held his gaze, refusing to flinch under the steely, penetrating glare he gave her. His eyes were like emerald fire, piercing her every secret. She felt incredibly grateful he couldn't read her mind, scour her heart and see her secret desires and worries.

"I know those cubs are more important right now," Callum agreed, "but that's not everything that seems to be running around that damned head of yours."

Sam shivered as Callum continued to study her carefully.

"What are you afraid of, Sammi?" he asked more softly, as if he really cared. Samantha steeled her resolve to resist this sexy man. He would surely unknowingly rip her battered heart to shreds given half the chance. He might mean well, might find her sexually appealing, but her heart simply couldn't afford to be devastated a second time. Samantha had already been burned once in the past, and she had no intention of repeating the experience again.

"I wouldn't have thought a woman like you would be scared of anything," he continued easily, concern mingled with a hungry curiosity shining brightly in his eyes.

Samantha *did* flinch at that.

"I'm scared of plenty of things, Callum. I just refuse to let anything as petty as being afraid ruin or change my life. Dinner will have been served by now, and frankly I don't want to have to answer awkward questions from Alexander, my father or my uncles. Do you?"

Callum smiled as he gently moved a few of her long curls behind her ear and adjusted the thin strap of her gown with the ease and familiarity of a man who had such a right.

"I think it would be fairly obvious to all and sundry what occurred out here," he commented, not without a bit of smug male pride. "But for now I'll let this slide. Understand this, though, Sammi—we haven't finished this conversation."

Samantha brushed past him to enter the door.

"We have if I say so," she said, enjoying having the parting shot for once.

As she re-entered the slightly stuffy ballroom, she could feel the heat of his eyes track her movements. Sitting down next to Alexander, she ignored her twin's curious and slightly amused look, just like she ignored the intensity of Callum's eyes upon her.

Raising her eyebrow to her twin arrogantly, knowing he at least wouldn't embarrass her in front of all their guests, she began to make polite conversation with the richly dressed matron seated on her other side.

The evening passed agonizingly slowly, and Samantha found her concentration shot to hell. She struggled valiantly to ignore the ache between her legs every time she felt Callum's eyes fall upon her, his gaze feeling hot and electric. More times than she cared to admit, she felt her attention straying to watch where Callum sat on the other side of the room, only to have her eyes skitter away when he, obviously also feeling her eyes on him, turned his burning gaze to meet hers.

As dessert was being brought forth, Samantha sighed internally, knowing as soon as her table had finished she could politely excuse herself. She also had a sneaking suspicion that now that the end of dinner was in sight, Alexander would not be denied too much longer.

"Tell me you didn't...do anything...out in the backyard," he whispered into her ear. She turned, a slight blush on her cheeks, but only anger in her eyes.

"Of course not," she hissed back at him. "I'm working with Callum. I'm supposed to be keeping an eye on him." Unfortunately, her angry, indignant whisper didn't upset her twin in the slightest. Worse still, as always, he could see right through her.

"He knows what we are, Sammi," Alexander said calmly, striking more fear into her heart than she could have possibly given him credit for. "You can't and won't be able to just throw him off like all your other lovers. And he's not anything like that dickhead Jonathon. He isn't going to use you to try to get a good story about the family and then dump you and break your heart."

"Damn you, Al," she said, her voice no less furious for all its softness. "What the hell do you think you're doing? How did he find out?"

When Alex just shrugged and dug into his rich double-chocolate cheesecake, Samantha could only sit there and try to sort out her conflicting emotions. After a moment of enjoying his cheesecake with more gusto and sinful indulgence than it deserved, Alex began to talk quietly with her once again.

"I told Bella a year ago or more. When Callum came to work with us on the wolf foundation, she asked if she could share the secret with him. I knew how special he is to her and saw no reason not to tell him. Why, darling sister? Is there a problem?"

Samantha stared at her twin, opened and then closed her mouth again. She refused to bare her soul any more to her twin tonight. Besides, likely he knew *exactly* what her problem with Callum knowing about her was.

If he were still interested in her, even knowing what she was and what she was capable of doing, it would be a million times harder for her to keep her distance and protect her heart from him. The speed and ease at which her desire was growing also didn't help her attempts to keep her distance. Alexander watched her, a twinkle in his eye, showing her that she was not concealing her desire for Callum at all well either.

Needing some time and privacy to sort herself out, Samantha stood up and politely gave her farewells to the table. As she pushed her chair back, she felt Alexander in her mind, the easy, comfortable mental conversation a special twins link they had shared their entire life.

Well done, Sammi. That was so calm and convincing I might have believed it myself.

Shut the hell up, she replied back with an unconvincing amount of force. She smiled and could feel his answering cheeriness. *Go...I don't know...kiss Bella or do something useful. I'll be in the office tomorrow morning to look over the files.*

She bent down to kiss her brother on the cheek and could feel his worry and concern for her as he stroked her bare shoulder. Standing back up and weaving her way between the tables once more, she could feel hot emerald eyes track her passage out of the room toward the front entrance.

She felt no surprise as a warm, solid hand came around her waist, holding her close while she waited for the valet to bring her small car around.

"Escaping, my dear? So unlike what I would have assumed of a strong, modern woman like yourself."

Samantha smiled at him. A part of her heart felt relieved that he knew about her being a werewolf, but her mind was in even more turmoil now.

"Ever heard of discretion being the better part of valor, chump?" she replied sassily. "What say we cut the crap and go look at those files now?" she added, needing to buy herself some space and time as well as wanting to take a small measure of control back for herself.

One golden brow arched and gave her a rush of smooth confidence. Samantha felt pleased with herself—she had obviously surprised him. She tried not to feel smug, but it was supremely difficult not to. She *loved* the thought she could put him off balance.

"Now?" Callum replied, a little startled. "You're really leaving?"

Samantha shrugged idly.

"It's either that or I..." She swallowed the sentence, long years of habit stilling the words in her mouth. It was then that Samantha realized that this was Callum and she could be honest with him. "I would go for a run," she said, slightly warily. "I need to clear my head. Both exercise and work do that for me."

She didn't want to add that she would have gone for a run in wolf form. She neither wanted to bring up *that* conversation here and now nor did she feel she needed to go into more detail. All that mess could wait until later.

Callum nodded, genuine understanding glinting in his eyes. Samantha smiled, but quickly wiped it from her mouth.

"Work it is then," he said easily, catching the smile before she could deny its presence. "As there is only one form of exercise I wish to do right now, and only one woman with whom I want to do it with, work might be the best current compromise."

Samantha could no longer hide her smile or the very faint blush which crossed her cheeks. She refused to rise to *that* bait either.

"I'll meet you at the offices then," she replied firmly, attempting to take back the control he seemed to so easily steal from her. "You have keys to the building, I assume?"

Callum nodded and patted his pants pocket. "Bella gave them to me last week when I finished my move."

As the valet brought her car around she turned to say goodbye, but found his lips lightly pressing down onto hers instead. She indulged her desire for a second or two, letting herself wallow in the feel of his mouth softly moving onto and over hers.

They pulled away simultaneously. Sam chortled at their almost identical expressions, both hungry for more but each of them wary of the intensity between them.

"Ten minutes?" he said, green eyes hot and roaming over her face.

Samantha nodded and climbed into her car. She hated driving in high heels, but the quicker she looked at the files, the quicker she could try to work out the million and one things in her head.

Waving to Callum as he stood in the half-light and watched her drive away, Samantha turned her favorite "I-am-not-depressed" CD on full volume and tried to let the music wash her mind clear.

She had a feeling she'd need all of her concentration to be in close confines with Callum and search for any evidence of what happened to those wolf cubs.

Chapter Five

ஐ

Samantha and Callum entered the reception area of the Rutledge Wolf Foundation. In the darkness, with the faint light from the street filtering in through the window, the place had an empty, eerie feel to it.

"Let's start with my office," Callum offered as he started to walk towards his area. "After that, if we're not completely exhausted, we can see if Bella or Alexander have any files that we should check through as well."

Samantha followed him through a door into a small office. Two desks sat on either side. A largely framed photo of Bella and Alexander hugging on a sunny day in the park graced one desk, upon which numerous neatly aligned piles of paper were stacked. The other desk was bare except for a pad of paper and a few scattered pens.

Callum must share his office with Bella, Samantha mused. She figured anything underhanded Callum could have possibly done must have occurred out in Australia. With the shared, open plan office, there was no way he could have had privacy to organize anything here without Bella or any of the other staff swiftly made aware of it. Callum had helped transport those cubs directly from Australia. He hadn't moved into his apartment and all his gear had still been shipping over when the event had taken place.

Before she could head over to the filing cabinet, she felt Callum standing next to her, positively radiating heat. She felt her breath hitch as she turned to face him and saw the hunger in his face. He pressed her against the back of the door, closing it as he ruthlessly took her mouth with his.

Callum felt almost all of his restraint dissolve as he finally allowed himself to unleash the pent-up need for this woman. Tilting his head, he opened her mouth and let his tongue slide in, licking and tasting her, almost feeling high on the pleasure coursing through his body at just the tangle of their tongues.

His hands were everywhere, looking for her hot spots and lingering over sensitive areas that had her shivering. Callum reveled in the little sounds of pleasure Samantha gave to him, intimate, erotic sounds only a lover would ever hear.

Growling, he felt the fire in him explode as she began to unbutton his tuxedo shirt, sliding a hand in to touch the hot skin of his chest. Unable to believe the strength of passion and heat this woman brought out in him, Callum had trouble restraining himself. He wrapped one arm around her waist, drawing her directly against the heated length of his body and, taking the bulk of her weight, pivoted on one foot and turned them both.

He now rested his back against the heavy wooden door and let both his hands wander freely around the silky material of her dress. Kissing her passionately, he felt amazement as he discovered the whole one side of her dress was split up the leg practically to her hip.

"How the hell do you walk in this thing and not flash everyone?" he asked hoarsely as he ran a hand inside the slinky material. He found no garters and no stockings, just naked, warm flesh underneath his hand. He palmed her ass, amazed to still feel nothing but the rounded, intimately soft flesh.

"Years of practice," he heard Sam whisper huskily as she strung kisses along his jaw.

As one hand busily pushed down the tiny, thin shoulder straps of her dress, the other roamed over her ass, finally finding a miniscule scrap of lace he assumed passed for a thong.

Women actually pay good money for a piece of lace that is so thin it feels like a single thread? Are they insane?

With a quick tug, Callum ripped the tiny piece of lace from her hips and looked at the scrap now limp in his hand. A wicked grin crossed his face as he noticed the red silk flowers daintily embroidered into the lacy motif, the shade matching the color of Samantha's sexy gown exactly.

Callum spent a few seconds imagining how it would have looked covering Samantha's pussy. The naughty visual gave him a small understanding of why women might enjoy wearing such tiny, teasing sets of panties.

Carefully, pace by pace, he walked them both across the room. Neither of them let go of the other. Halfway across the office he lost his jacket and shirt, moaning at the immense pleasure Samantha gave him as she traced her fingers delicately over his pecs and her fingernail flicked his nipple.

Callum managed to find the slim zipper on her side, pull it free and push her dress down from her chest and over her hips. He looked at the lacy scrap of thong still in his hand and carefully placed it in his pants pocket. Finally they made it to the soft couch Bella had shown him with such pride a week or so before. He had seen his cousin interviewing people on it, insisting the couch was a far more intimate and comfortable arrangement than chairs could hope to be.

Better business, she had blithely assured him.

Callum hadn't really understood the difference between a couch and a few comfortable armchairs, but he swore to thank Bella for her foresight the following day.

Samantha pulled herself free and Callum had to fist his hands, which automatically itched to grab her back. He restrained himself, as he didn't get the feeling that this luscious woman was attempting to run from him.

Proving his instinct right, Samantha merely took a few steps backward and fell down gracefully onto the couch, splaying her legs wide and looking for all the world like a sexy siren beckoning him to his death.

The moonlight washed over her pale body, and he knew he had never seen such beauty in all his years.

With a mocking glint in her eye, she raised one red-stilettoed foot to prop against the arm of the couch. She waited patiently for him, her eyes hot and wicked.

Callum kicked off his own shoes, impatiently pulled at his socks and carelessly left them where they fell. Knowing if he removed his pants and boxer briefs the game would be over long before their time, he kept the rest of his clothes on and stepped toward the gorgeous woman in front of him. Kneeling on the floor before her, he caressed her ankles as he unstrapped the sparkly buckle.

"A man on his knees, exactly where I love them," she purred sensually.

Unbelievably, he felt his cock tighten and harden even more. Incredibly grateful that he had had the foresight to not remove his pants. Otherwise he would have spread her legs and plunged balls-deep into her right then and to hell with her sandals.

"You'll have your turn, Sammi," he promised, conviction resonating in his voice. "I think we'll both spend plenty of time on our knees, don't you?"

While she merely grinned, he carefully unbuckled the other stiletto, placing both of them safely underneath the couch where they wouldn't get trod upon later.

Finally, he was free to indulge himself. He allowed himself to relax his control and do what he had been impatient to do since the second he had seen her. He spread her legs wide and gazed in rapt enjoyment at her heavily weeping pussy.

Neatly clipped brown hair covered her secrets, the pearly colored cream drawing him to her slit like a beacon. Holding a tight, fierce grip on his self-control, wanting to give her more pleasure than any man ever had or could in the future, he brought his face right up to the apex of her thighs and licked her slowly, savoring the flavor and texture of her outer lips.

He ran his tongue gently up over her folds, separating the pouting lips tenderly. He gloried in her moan, enjoyed the way she shifted her hips so he had better access to her swollen pussy.

She was so damp, so swollen, that he knew without a doubt she had been thinking about this, been hot and waiting for his sexual possession for hours. No woman could be this ready, this needy in a few mere minutes of foreplay.

No, his Samantha had been working herself up through the dinner, and maybe even been far more effected by their tryst in the garden than he had previously understood. He filed away the thought that Samantha seemed to be attempting to hide many of her physical responses to him.

He inhaled her scent, a spicy, utterly feminine smell of musky need. As he lapped at her juices, he rolled the unique taste around his mouth, thinking how grateful he was that at least in this manner, she couldn't lie or hide from him.

"You taste delicious, Sammi," he said huskily, reluctant to move away from her even to say this. "Like ambrosia."

She laughed softly and raised her arms above her head, letting them hang over the edge of the couch. The gesture of feminine surrender fired him up even further, made him feel potently masculine and like a conquering hero.

Callum returned his head to her apex, stroked a finger over her clit and dived back to lap at her offerings. He watched her, mesmerized by the way her long, dark curls fell, the sleepy, lazy burn of her dark blue eyes. Her breasts were full, heavy, pale brown nipples peaked and begging for his attention.

Enjoying the way Samantha moaned and twisted to give him easier access, Callum raised his other hand so both could now toy and play with her lush body.

"Callum," she panted, and he knew she needed more, but he wanted to draw this first time between them out as long as physically possible. He felt a deep-seated need to bring her everything he could. He continued to play with her nipple and clit, lapped her steadily flowing slit more quickly, running his tongue over her swollen, sensitive flesh.

He paused, amazed, as he felt her hands reach his shoulders and try to draw him upward and closer to her body.

"I need you right now. I can't wait any longer," she panted, and he felt his heart swell and overflow. He released her nipple and kissed her fiercely, letting her taste herself on his lips.

With no warning, and knowing none was needed, as wet and swollen as she was, he thrust two fingers deeply inside her.

Samantha cried out, and he swallowed the sound hungrily, rubbed her clit and stroked the inside of her tightly clenching walls. He looked at her and he could *see* it in her eyes when the climax ripped through her. Her eyes went a deeper shade of blue, shock and surprise lying in their depths.

She screamed, making herself cut the sound off as she pressed her lips together.

"No," he panted. "Don't close it off, give those sounds to me. I love to hear them."

He continued to stroke her, and she closed her eyes, arched her neck and moaned deeply, a harsh sound torn from her soul.

Callum smiled as he continued to softly pet her until her breathing returned to normal. For a moment they just rested there in each other's arms, breathing in one another's scents until Samantha tilted her head up and opened her eyes, stared directly at him.

"I do believe it's your turn now," she said softly, melting his heart even more.

"Are you sure?" he asked carefully, wanting her to be fully aware of all the ramifications of them doing this together. "Because if we do this, then there's no running away again. I won't let you. If you have even the slightest doubts, Sammi, you better stop us right now. I won't mind."

Yeah. Right, his mind sneered, but Callum pushed the thought away.

He'd be lying if he said he didn't want to finish this, but he felt adamant it would be Samantha's choice. If they had sex now she would be making a commitment to him and that was final. He freely gave her the choice, but once she made it, he would not let her back out from it.

From the way she paused, looked him over, he knew she understood exactly where he was coming from. When she nodded and smiled at him, he felt his whole body relax with the relief.

Chapter Six

✍

Callum watched, utterly amazed as Samantha spread her legs invitingly, widening his view of her pussy. When she reached up, fumbled with the odd fastenings of his tux pants, he laughed softly. He reached down, rested his fingers on hers and showed her how to free him from the restriction of his clothes.

He felt fully charged and as eager as a schoolboy. There was just something about this time, something about Samantha, that made him feel as if this was particularly special, particularly precious.

As they undid the clasps and unzipped his fly, he stripped his shirt from his body, then let Samantha tug his pants down to the floor. He stood in front of her, naked as the day he was born. He let her look her fill, her eyes hungrily searching over his body, resting and widening slightly at his thick, erect staff.

He had never been one to compare himself to others, but he could feel how impressed Samantha was, and he let a purely masculine satisfaction rush over him for just a moment. He climbed onto the couch and gently stroked her face. His cock leaked a tiny pearl of pre-come, and he knew he wouldn't be able to last long.

"This time will have to be fast, baby. I'm sorry, but I want you too much."

When Samantha smiled, laughed lightly and wrapped her arms around his neck, he felt himself tense up even more in preparation for his explosion.

"I am not delicate or a virgin, Cal. I am more than happy to mix the rough with the gentle."

Callum bent down and kissed her softly, gently, wanting her to experience the awe and incredible pleasure he too felt.

"I won't break," she whispered softly against his lips, and he felt his restraint disappear as if it had never been there.

She wrapped her legs around his waist, and with a hand on her hip to guide himself, he plunged his cock deeply inside her. She arched into him, accepting him fully, and Callum felt his heart melt and fly into her small, delicate hands. She embraced him, accepted him, pushed him for more and more and he knew he would never get over her.

Holy shit, I've fallen in love! he realized, not without a large dose of surprise.

Callum drew Samantha up to him, pulled her as closely as he could. He angled himself so he rubbed her clit as he thrust in and out of her gloving heat. Kissing her fiercely, desperately yearning for more, Callum licked and ate at her mouth. With the new realization of love clear in his head, he needed everything he could get from her.

Mindful of the slimness of the couch, Callum held Samantha tightly to him. Restricting her movements only seemed to inflame them both even more. She ravaged his mouth, tangled her tongue with his and seemed to draw from him everything he could offer.

He held himself firmly in check, grazing her clit in the desperate hope she could find her pleasure before he lost his mind. He felt Samantha stiffen under him and he halted, worried for a moment he had hurt her somehow.

"Don't...stop..." she gasped, and he realized she had been even closer to the edge than he had understood. He withdrew from her slowly, letting her savor the friction, and then he plunged into her as deeply as he could once more.

Samantha screamed and he could feel the sound being ripped from her, tearing through her body. He felt the contractions of her pussy clenching around himself, and stilling, he waited a few seconds to allow the exquisite sensation milk his thick, hard shaft.

A moment later, Samantha's body began to relax, all the tension of her climax seeping out of her body, leaving it boneless. The lazy smile, the sparkle in her eyes let him know she had found her satisfaction. As if he had been released from a spell, Callum let himself go, pumped into her only a few more times before he shouted his own release, spilling his seed deeply inside her and filling her with his essence.

Exhilarated, Callum pulled Samantha even closer to him, crushing her against his chest and gently bit down on her neck as he pumped himself into her over and over.

A second later, he felt as if all the energy and air left him, and he collapsed on her. When she shifted under him, he made a face and carefully turned let his body drop to the floor and pulled Samantha on top of him, and then rolled her under him once more.

He desperately willed himself to magically become erect again, but his body refused to accommodate him. Callum honestly couldn't remember the last time he had indulged in such all-consuming sex. Certainly he had never bellowed like that before, never felt his ejaculation go on and on.

It would be at least a little while before his body let him repeat the experience.

With Samantha panting and lying beneath him, he let his body relax and enjoy the feel of her.

Chapter Seven

໓

Samantha lay panting. Her entire body felt lax, utterly sapped of all its energy. She honestly couldn't remember when she had either enjoyed sex more or had had such an astonishingly fantastic orgasm.

"Goddess," she whispered softly, mostly to herself, still not fully having her breath back. When Callum only chuckled and rolled the bulk of his weight onto his side, her hands reached for his shoulders of their own volition, instantly wanting him covering her once again. She bit her lip, wondering what the hell she should do now.

She was supposed to be finding the missing cubs, not to mention proving to Alexander that Callum had absolutely nothing to do with their disappearance, but instead she was indulging—again!—with knock-your-socks-off, mind-blowing sex with Callum.

"Goddess," she whispered again as she squeezed her eyes shut. She needed to get a grip on herself, needed to get to work on finding the poor cubs and returning them to where they belonged.

"You know," Callum said, still rather breathless, "in anyone else, that kind of stunned mindlessness would sound good. But I have a feeling you're not swearing over how wonderful that just was."

Samantha opened her eyes and looked deeply into her lover's green eyes.

My lover, her mind resonated, stuck for a moment on that heart-stopping information.

How right it sounded. How utterly perfect. Problem was, there was still a mound of things between them that they needed to talk about, and right now the only thing she wanted was cast-iron proof that he was free and clear and someone else was responsible for the kidnapping of the two cubs.

"What is it? You're not stressing about protection, are you? I know you're clean, and I swear I am too."

Samantha squeezed her eyes shut again. She did not want this conversation. They might be both clean, but she now knew beyond a shadow of a doubt that he was her True Mate, and so she could still become pregnant.

They could get pregnant.

Samantha stood up and stalked out of the office. Opening the private connecting door, she strode through into Alexander's office. She knew he kept a gym bag in his wardrobe, and Samantha desperately needed to put some clothes on, to get some distance.

This whole…whatever it could be called…had been a complete mess from start to finish. How was she supposed to keep an eye on Callum, to watch his investigation and find out what the hell was going on when she was screwing him and falling more and more desperately in love with him every minute?

In love? her mind echoed, panic beginning to gnaw on the edge of her conscious.

She recoiled in horror from her own thoughts. Throwing open the door to the closet, Samantha pushed aside the two spare suits Alexander kept there until she found the soft gym bag on the bottom.

Hefting it easily, she slammed it down on the desk as her thoughts circled around madly. Ripping the bag open, she removed the sweatpants and baggy T-shirt from its depths. Alexander's sneakers were way too large for her, but she pulled on the socks after sniffing them to make sure they were clean. The less flesh she had exposed to Callum MacLennon, the safer she would be.

Just as she was carelessly throwing the nearly empty bag onto a crumpled heap on the floor of her twin's closet, Callum stalked through the door. He had put his tuxedo pants back on and his shirt was unbuttoned.

He also looked royally pissed off.

"I don't know what it is about you, Sammi," he said angrily, but obviously attempting to calm himself down out of his temper, "but you manage to piss me off and make me burn for you simultaneously. Why the hell is that?"

She tried to dodge him as he closed the distance between them. She thought maybe if she could keep the desk between them then she could keep herself under control and maybe she could go back to pretending this man didn't touch her heart and soul.

As usual, Callum paid no attention to what she tried to do. Instead, he jumped up onto the desk and easily dropped down the other side to where she stood frozen and gently grabbed her arm.

He kissed her. Possessively, fiercely, and despite herself she could feel the cream gathering once more in her bare pussy and her bones begin to melt.

When he pulled roughly away from her, she opened her eyes, dazed. Callum groaned in frustration, even though his body still hummed with pleasure and desire.

"How the hell can we share that fire, passion and overwhelming desire for each other," he asked, "but you still won't trust me?"

Samantha took a slow, deep breath. "We have to find those cubs," she started shakily, willing herself to not answer the hurt and need flaring in his deep green eyes. "I need to go over the information, right now."

When Callum frowned, she knew he wouldn't give up without a fight.

"Of course we are going to find the cubs," he agreed. Sam smiled until he continued, "Bella told me to help you out and to watch over you, do what I can to help the investigation along. That doesn't explain—"

Samantha cut him off, her mind whirling.

"Bella told you to watch over me?" she asked, astonished.

Callum seemed to notice her complete change of mood, and, surprisingly, he took it easily in stride. "Yeah, at the dinner. Just before you came up to me. Why?"

Samantha had started to pace without even realizing it. She bit her lip and concentrated. The situation felt like too much of a coincidence—Bella suggesting Callum watch over her *and* Alex implicating Callum in the loss of the cubs, thus insisting she keep an eye on Callum. Alexander, of course, had known exactly how to go about piquing her interest and seeking her help with the investigation.

Alexander would know very well that the twin temptations of watching over Callum and searching for the cubs would have had her undivided attention. Now knowing Bella had been telling Callum to watch over *her*, the chances were high her twin and his fiancée were up to something together.

"Alexander told me almost exactly the same thing—but with a slightly different twist. Let's look at those files. There just has to be something interesting there."

"What do you mean a twist?" Callum said, his voice echoing in the still evening air as she left him in Alexander's office. She crossed over to his filing cabinet and started opening the drawers.

"Hang on, Bella is a fiend when it comes to the filing, let me get it," he insisted, pushing past her and gingerly sorting through the color-coded, alphabetized files.

Samantha waited while Callum carefully sifted through a few manila envelopes and then pull out some sheaves of paper. Grabbing the files he offered to her, she sat cross-legged on the floor and spread the sheets out before her. Quickly, she glanced through them and began to separate them into piles.

She didn't notice she had blocked everything out until Callum waved a hand in front of her face, obviously trying to gain her attention.

"...hello?" Callum's voice penetrated her deep thoughts.

"Sorry? I'm concentrating. Callum, look here." She waved a few sheets of paper in her hand and smiled as he sat down next to her on the floor to look over her shoulder. Pointing to the relevant sections she had discovered, she showed him the import reports and receipts.

"I'm not going to get anything out of you until after you've searched these papers, right?" Callum said as he grinned wryly back at her.

"Right," she agreed distantly, her mind working quickly she began to fire off question after question, picking his brain for every last contact, every last detail he could recall.

She pushed all of her jumbled thoughts to the back of her mind. She also courageously attempted to forget the scorchingly hot memories of make-you-beg sex. It would only detract from her attention.

Instead, Samantha concentrated fully on doing the job she had promised her brother—clearing this mess up. After the situation was resolved, *then* she could allow herself to decide where exactly it was she stood with her lover.

Chapter Eight

ဢ

Callum wearily rubbed a hand over his face. He had never seen this side of Samantha. He had seen her grumpy, wary, angry and being pushed to the erotic edge, but he had never seen just how single-minded she could be when she focused her mind on a task.

He couldn't help but admit privately that he found it fascinating to see this side of his woman.

My woman.

He had met her twice, fucked her senseless and already he felt as if they belonged together. He had scoffed when Bella had sighed and declared she had fallen in love the moment she had seen Alexander. How the very first time they made love they had both known they belonged together forever. He had thought it pure romantic nonsense.

Did Samantha feel the same way he did?

He could understand her wariness. She was such an independent, modern woman that it made sense she not want to let any man in too quickly. Yet much as his gut had informed him that Bella had been keeping something from him at the dinner, so too did he feel most strongly that there was something else nagging on the edges of Samantha's mind.

"Ah-HA!" she cried out, scattering papers everywhere on the floor. Callum smiled, relieved she had found something. His mind had shut down over half an hour ago. He looked at his watch.

Shit! Nearly three a.m.!

"What did you find, baby? My eyes started crossing a while ago."

"Look here. Monique Thomason signed for the cubs when they handed them over to her! I couldn't make out the scrawl earlier. I *knew* he had to have something to do with this. It was all just too pat."

Callum frowned, not sure if Samantha was speaking gibberish or if he really was just so tired her words weren't making sense.

"He? But Monique—"

"Is a woman's name. My middle name. Thomas is Alexander's middle name. When we were kids and needed aliases—or an imaginary friend to blame some mishap on to our parents—we always came up with Monique Thomason. We thought we were so clever." He watched as she chuckled and shook her head. "Our parents could see right through us the whole time. I don't know how they coped with the both of us."

Callum frowned, his mind clicking into gear.

"But if Alexander signed for these, or even if someone signed this form *for* him..."

His eyes widened as the possibilities hit him. Samantha's eyes were also large, showing she was likely thinking the same as he. "Then Alexander and likely Bella were in on this from the beginning. Which leads me back to where I started from. When Alexander called me, he told me to keep an eye on you too. He said he wanted me to closely watch every move you make, as it was your project. He wondered if...well..."

Callum felt anger sear through him. "Your brother thought *I* had something to do with this?"

He felt a cool, light hand touch his wrist. Samantha had stood up and crossed over to where he sat.

"No, I think he was baiting me, piquing my interest. He knew between two missing wolf cubs and you being under suspicion I wouldn't let up, that I'd follow you around like the lamest of puppy dogs. In my professional opinion..." Callum felt his cock rise back to attention as she lowered her voice and leaned into him, her chest pressed enticingly against his, her lips mere inches from his ear and neck.

His pulse pounded as she continued. "In my professional opinion, Callum, I do believe we have been set up."

"Really?" he croaked hoarsely, all his blood having headed south and his brain scrambling to keep up with what she said. He tried to gauge how Samantha felt about this. Personally, a part of Callum was pissed off at such a juvenile setup that could have easily ended in disaster. Truth be told, though, he was too happy with Samantha to bother reaming his cousin right now.

"So where do we go from here?" he asked softly, searching Samantha's face and eyes intently.

He looked deeply into the bluest eyes he had ever found, knowing exactly what he wanted to do now. The pole wedged in his poor tuxedo pants clearly explained where his mind was at.

"I am going to seriously kick my brother's ass," she said fiercely. Callum was trying to figure how to reply to that when she continued, "But without his and Bella's scheming it might have taken us both so much longer to sort this out for ourselves. That doesn't negate the fact they both deserve to be yelled at—but I think I'm feeling too satisfied to be bothered right now."

Samantha smiled and kissed his cheek, grabbed his shoulders and sat him up. Callum beamed, elation washing through him.

"I do believe it's time to go home."

"Mine or yours?" he asked, scrambling for his shoes.

"Mine," she said as she bent to pick up her stilettos from under the couch and the crumpled mass that had been her sexy red dress from the floor. He admired the wonderful picture of her bent ass and licked his lips.

"Brilliant," he said as they linked hands and exited the office.

He barely registered leaving the building, reactivating the alarms and fumbling for his keys. Callum memorized her address when she whispered it into his ear and then dropped his keys when she kissed him fully, pulling his body flush with her own.

The cold feeling of being left behind crept over him when Samantha pulled away, swaying her luscious ass as she stalked to her own car and climbed in.

When the roar of the engine snapped him back into reality, he jumped into his truck and peeled out after her.

Damned if he'd let her get away from him, even for the few minutes it would take to get to her apartment.

Chapter Nine

Samantha pulled her car into a parking spot at her apartment. She climbed out of the car, feeling naughty but slightly strange, having no panties on. Before she had even shut her car door, she heard the sound of Callum walking up the path to her front door. She smiled, slammed and locked her door, and turned to meet him.

He looked hungry, ravenous, almost. She seriously doubted it had been a long time since he had last had sex, not including what they had already shared tonight, but he still managed to look as if he were a horny teenager who had just discovered the joys of sex.

"You look like a man who has been celibate for years," she said with a small smile. Around you, sweetheart," he said huskily, making her shiver at his words, "that's rather like how I feel. I'm certainly no saint, but you seem to bring out the insatiable sinner in me."

Samantha opened her door and turned back to smile cheekily at him.

"That's quite a compliment there, sailor. Care to come on board?"

She felt her knees go weak as he grinned wickedly at her, placed one large palm around her waist and led them both through the open door.

"I thought you'd never ask," he murmured as he kicked the door shut with his foot.

Samantha forgot all about the deadbolt or alarm. Every thought flew from her mind as she fell headfirst into his devastating kiss. She cupped his face in both hands, angling his head so she could spear her tongue into his welcoming mouth.

Callum pulled Alexander's huge T-shirt over her head and a mere touch from his hands had the sweats falling to her feet. Her dress and stilettos were still strewn carelessly on the floor of her car.

She shrugged, utterly unconcerned. There were always other dresses, other stores to visit. Although she loved that particular dress, it didn't hold any interest to her at this moment.

She wrestled with Callum's pants, urgently needing to strip them from his body, only to discover him trying to toe off his shoes. His socks weren't on, obviously left behind in the office somewhere. Samantha giggled at the thought of the morning cleaners finding a pair of stray socks when they came in to wash the floors.

"It's never a good indication when a woman giggles as a man is being undressed."

"Sorry," she said, her hands eagerly helping his black boxer briefs to slide over his hips. "I was thinking of the cleaning crew finding your socks."

He snickered as well. "I am very glad they don't give reports to Alexander, Bella, Christiana or Edward. Bedroom?"

Samantha didn't believe she could live a moment longer without tasting his lips again. She held his hand and pulled his face closer to kiss deeply. Slowly, she led them to her bedroom. Before she could even enter through the doorway, he had picked her up and carried her to the bed.

She started, surprised. She didn't think any man had picked her up since she had been a little girl. After a second, she looked deeply into the green eyes that bored into her own.

"You're full of surprises, aren't you?" she said, enjoying the feeling of being soft and feminine. She couldn't recall the last lover whom she had felt so mushy over.

She felt her breath hitch at his devastating smile, as if she were the only woman in the world he felt an interest in. Truly those eyes should be outlawed, or at the very least classified as a weapon of mass destruction.

She could feel her every insecurity, her every utterly logical reason why she would never mate, never have a partner, crumble to the ground and become dust in his wake.

She had fallen utterly and irrevocably in love.

"I hope to be surprising you every day for the rest of our lives," Callum promised huskily, his green eyes deep and dark with hidden secrets and soul-deep promises.

Samantha sucked in a breath and wondered if the madness of the moment had fully overtaken her. "You shouldn't say things like that. It seemed perilously close to a proposal."

"Well." White teeth flashed in the semidarkness. Samantha laughed softly as she was casually dropped onto the bed. Seconds later, Callum's hard, warm body was pressing down on hers. "I wouldn't want to steal Bella's thunder or anything, and I don't have a ring yet, but I know my mind. I might have been on the other side of the world, but it's you who's been running away emotionally all these months. I'd have been more than happy to take that first night between us much, much further if you'd have let me."

Samantha laughed and rolled him over, straddled him. "I never run," she insisted, with her nose stuck in the air. "I merely made a strategic retreat to regroup. I do, however, seem to have been overcome."

Samantha closed her mouth, firmly biting on her lip. She wasn't prepared just yet to tell him she loved him. It seemed too intimate, too private to share for the moment.

And so instead she scooted down the bed, opened her mouth and took him within her, as much of him as could fit in her mouth. Her eyes fluttered shut, his salty, tangy taste overwhelming her senses, the masculine, woodsy scent of him washing over her as if she had dived into him.

She didn't hear his moan of approval, but she could feel the flex of his muscles, see the sheets move as he clenched them in his fist. She wrapped one palm lightly around the rest of his length, a marvelously impressive length it was too, and she suckled him. Her tongue explored, finding all the hidden nerves, washing over the tiny slit of his eye, lapping and laving at the sensitive skin.

It almost felt as if there was white noise in her head. All Samantha was aware of was their pleasure, the way both their bodies moved in tandem. She could feel the burning need in him as it grew and grew and she pressed harder into him, wanting to sate and satisfy him, give him as much pleasure as he gave her.

Her fingers tickled over his skin, rubbing and caressing the veins there. Flicking her tongue out, she explored his head, eagerly lapping the tiny amount of pre-come.

Time seemed to stand still and paradoxically rush forward at the same time. When she felt Callum's warm hands cup her face and pull her upward, she smiled and allowed it.

"I need to taste myself on you," he muttered huskily as he reached for her. "I need to have you right now, Sammi."

She nodded breathlessly as he kissed her and rolled her over on the large bed. Her legs spread wide of their own volition, as eager as he to start their endgame. Grabbing his waist, she aligning him with herself, and they both moaned as he thrust deeply into her, penetrating her and bringing them as close together as possible.

Samantha felt her hips arch as one of his hands stroked over her clit, sending the already burning fire roaring through her system. She canted her hips in time to his thrusts, needing more and more with every breath. The wave of her climax built quickly inside her, the energy rising and her breaths coming short and fast. Simultaneously she wanted to ride its crest forever but also to lose herself in the swell of the moment. She knew she couldn't have it both ways, and so she did the next best thing.

With a small grunt from the effort, Samantha flipped them over again, straddled Callum and thrust herself down heavily on the whole length of his cock. She rose and fell to the rhythm in her own soul, riding him hard and fast.

Callum's cock penetrated her deeply, but her spirit, her soul felt the rise of the strong love between them also growing. The physical pleasure mingled with the heightened emotions she could feel swirling between them, and they almost seemed to feed from one another.

Samantha felt herself slip slightly out of control, she had the overwhelming sensation to bite him, to mark him as hers forever.

Never, *ever* before had she felt this need, the desire to mark anyone. She had never even come close. Not only was it a mark of ownership, it also went far deeper than that. It was a commitment, a showing of love and devotion.

It was as binding as marriage vows and as public to others of her kind as wearing a ring. It was something she had *sworn* to never do, and something she had never even had the tiniest tingling of wanting.

Until now.

Not fully wanting to, but also not having the strength to resist properly, she bent her head to Callum's long neck. She kissed him, tenderly licked the spot where she wanted desperately to mix their essences.

With a huge force of will, with every cell inside her crying out in denial, she pulled away and continued to press herself up and down Callum's cock.

Sex should be enough, she told herself sternly. *It was always enough.*

It always had been enough, another part of her mind insisted. *Obviously it no longer is, darling.*

"Do it," she heard him whisper, hoarse with his desire for her.

Samantha shook her head, knowing he had no idea what she really wanted.

"Damn it, Sammi," he exploded, strain visible on his face as he gallantly held off his own climax, waiting for her. "You know we belong together and I know what you want to do. Mark me. Just do it, damn you."

For a moment she paused, held them both on the knife-edge of satisfaction.

"How the hell—"

"Bella," he said softly. "She told me. I recognized what you wanted. I want it too. I love you, Sammi."

Samantha felt her heart cave in and fly into his hands for always. She knew they would have problems, they would probably argue and scream and she might be tempted to throw things at him.

But they loved each other with a heartfelt devotion, and that was the only place to ever start a lifetime of commitment like this.

She thrust back down upon him so hard they both moaned, her cunt clasping him so tightly she felt amazed he wasn't in pain. He felt even thicker inside her now, if possible.

Samantha barely noticed as he rolled her onto her back. She had wrapped her hands around his neck, pulling him so closely to her that their flesh pressed into one another. Long legs were wrapped around his waist as he held her hips at an angle and penetrated her even more deeply.

Callum cried out as Samantha gently bit into his neck. Even in the heat and passion of the moment Samantha knew *exactly* what it was she did, what she was committing to and what she was promising him. From the hungry, possessive look in his dark green eyes, Callum too understood what they were sharing.

As she bit down into tender skin, she felt her pussy begin to contract. Concentrating, Samantha pulled a tiny amount of his scent from him and gave him her heart, her soul and her essence—*her* scent. She mingled them together, bound her heart to him forever.

And she let go to allow the earth-shattering orgasm wash over her.

She felt herself contract over and over, felt her body reach out and clasp him so tightly to her he might have bruises the following morning. Callum plunged into her in short, hard thrusts, pushing himself over his own peak, only to have him explode inside her and shoot his seed deeply inside her body.

Screaming, Samantha arched into him, her mind fuzzy with the pleasure he gave her. The sensation of him filling her, stretching her so tightly, was exquisite and something she hoped neither of them would ever take for granted or tire of.

Callum's now familiar weight fell on top of her, and Samantha held her lover close, enjoying the solid feel of him, the tangy sweat beading his body, his intoxicating scent and the very faint floral fragrance of her own scent underlying his own.

Smiling sleepily, she gently nuzzled his neck as he rolled from her, spooned her from behind. She wrapped his arms around her, ducking out only for a split second to pull the covers over them both.

"Tomorrow, or rather later today," he whispered into her neck sleepily, "we need to have a serious chat with your brother and my cousin."

"Yeah," she said happily, letting the heat of his embrace and his wonderful scent wash over her. "But it's going to be hard to act annoyed with them. I would have continued to avoid you for months, if not years, if Alex hadn't pushed me along."

"Never would have happened. I was making plans of my own."

"Oh?" she said sleepily, yawning delicately.

"Yeah, baby," he rumbled, sleep making his voice thick and even more potently sexy. "I was going to hire you on any one of a dozen pretexts."

Samantha smiled as she felt Callum begin to fall asleep behind her. She wriggled closer into his embrace, happy beyond measure.

"Once I found out you knew about my wolf side and knew many of our secrets, I wouldn't have put up much of a fight. You're just too damn sexy."

"Good to hear," he murmured. Samantha could practically hear him slide into a deep, restful sleep.

She laughed softly, held him tightly around her and closed her eyes, a deep, peaceful sleep overtaking her.

Epilogue
A few months later…

ജ

Samantha felt ready to scream.

"Mom, if you don't get out of here and let me be, I swear to heaven I will not be responsible for my actions."

"For a blushing bride, you sure are cranky, darling," her mother said cheerily, still fussing with Sam's long curly hair.

While Bella had a huge white gown, two frilly petticoats underneath, a floor-length veil and delicate pink roses in her hair, Samantha had gone for a simple knee-length dress in ivory, a few wildflowers twisted in her dark locks and a handful of her Aunt Sophie's cornflowers clenched tighter than necessary in her hand.

Sam utterly refused to admit that she was nervous as hell. Bella had been throwing up all morning. Nerves, she insisted, though privately Sam felt certain that Bella was pregnant.

She, however, had no such excuse for her nerves or for the two times she had herself thrown up before the hordes of family and friends had descended on her to "make her radiant".

A knock at the door gave her the perfect excuse to move away from her fussing mother. If she didn't get out of here soon, she'd say something awful she would regret later on. Somehow, Sam just wanted to be left alone to fret in private.

When she opened the door to her Uncle Dominic, she felt so relieved that she didn't tease him when his grin widened at her.

"How is the gorgeous bride?" he asked as he loosened his bow tie and made a comedic face at her to express the lengths he was going for her.

Samantha grabbed her uncle's hand and led him outside the small cabin.

"I am going crazy. Take me on a walk."

She half dragged him away from the cabin, ignoring her mother's frustrated yells for her to come back or she'd ruin her hair and makeup. Her mother was more than capable to take over for the last of the pre-wedding preparations. Besides, there was more than an hour left.

Leading Dominic into the familiarity of the woods, Samantha felt herself calm down with each step that brought her further away from the prissy mess back at the main house.

"I'm not helping you jilt the poor guy, am I, Sammi?" Dominic grinned as he teased her.

Samantha smiled in return, but replied honestly. "No, Uncle Dom. I just need to breathe. Bella is...a bit fretful." Samantha had to swallow the news of her sister-in-law's pregnancy. "It's all such a buzz in there—I can't breathe. I know I'm doing the right thing, but I've never wanted a huge white wedding. I never really wanted *any* wedding.

"Dom, I love Callum, but why the hell do I need to go through with this? He knows I love him, knows I've marked him. I'll happily wear his rings. I just don't think I can do this."

Samantha continued to walk through the forest, each section as familiar as her own face. She had grown up here, played forever in these woods, run here every month for as long as she could remember. She felt the wind in her face and she could scent each individual flower as she passed it.

Finally, she came to a glade that she had often dreamed in, spent alone time in, as a child. Samantha hadn't been purposely heading here, or not consciously anyway, but somehow it felt *right* being here as she closed one chapter on her life and opened a new one.

After a rather heated discussion about her twin's matchmaking skills, or lack thereof, the entire mess with the "kidnapped" cubs had been laid to rest. The cubs had been safe and secreted away, both Bella and Alexander had been taking good care of them. It had also been near to impossible to chew her brother a new asshole when he continued to smirk about how deeply in love she had fallen with Callum.

Bella too had been ecstatic that everything had fallen into place so perfectly, and it had been her idea to have a double wedding. Samantha had hesitated at first, mostly because she knew the large, white, traditional wedding was one of Bella's dreams, and she didn't want to dampen Bella's enthusiasm.

Everything had been working perfectly, she had never been as happy as she was with Callum and they were both madly, irrevocably in love, and yet something niggled in the back of her mind, something she seemed to be missing. With a strangled cry, Samantha dropped down onto a particularly grassy spot and started sobbing. She felt even more grateful as Dominic merely sat down beside her, uncaring of the stains probably gathering on his tux. He didn't touch her or coddle her, but let her sob her worries out.

After a moment, she turned away from her uncle, dry retched, and felt a strange, calming peace settle over herself. She turned back, smiled weakly at the worried expression on Dom's face, sighed and leaned on Dom's strong shoulder, and he finally put a warm, soothing arm around her.

"You do realize you're pregnant, don't you, Sammi?" Samantha chuckled again at the casual, almost disinterested way her uncle said this. "Mary was incredibly hormonal with the first baby. Seems to be a running theme in Rutledge women."

"I can't be," she said softly, wondering… She placed a hand on her flat stomach and closed her eyes, breathing deeply. Searching inside herself, Samantha smiled, almost certain her uncle was wrong, until she found two tiny little beings.

Completely shocked, Samantha choked, gasped and placed her other hand over her first to make absolutely certain she wasn't mistaken.

Utterly disbelieving, she sat there as the minutes ticked by, utterly lost in the joy of the little beings she and Callum had made in their love.

"If you're really that panicked over the wedding, why not get the priest to come out here and marry you? I seriously doubt Bella or Alex would mind, and you know Callum is so besotted with you he'd agree to almost anything."

Samantha looked up to her uncle and burst into tears again, throwing both her arms around him and holding him tight. "Do you really think so, Uncle Dom? Are you sure Callum won't mind?"

"I know I sure as hell don't mind," a familiar voice came from behind her. "I'll do anything you want if you just stop crying, Sammi."

Samantha raised her head from her uncle's shoulder and stared, amazed to find Alexander and Callum just entering the small glade.

"Callum! It's bad luck—"

"Alexander could feel how upset you were. It scared the shit out of me, so fuck tradition. I think we'll manage just fine without it, Sammi. Why didn't you tell me you were upset?"

"I wasn't until just now. It all just kinda came crashing down on me."

Samantha sniffed, wiped the tears from her eyes and stood up. Smiling at how handsome Callum looked in his tux, she walked over him. If possible, he looked even more handsome than he had on that fateful night at the wolf foundation dinner.

Damn, her man rocked in a tux.

"I've been a bit odd these last few days," she explained softly, reaching out to take Callum's hand. "I thought it was just stress from the wedding, the planning and not being as into it as I thought I should be. But Callum." Samantha felt her spirit lift and her eyes glow with happiness as they twined their fingers through each other's.

She took a deep breath, wanting to let this memory linger forever in her mind. "We're having twins," she said softly, enjoying the shock and happiness cross over her lover's face.

Samantha grinned widely as Callum drew her closer to him, cherished the stunned amazement on his face. She watched with awe as he reached out his free hand and placed it carefully on her stomach.

"We're having a baby?" he repeated. "Two babies, even? You shouldn't be out here," Callum fretted, causing Samantha to smile even more widely. "You should be inside. What if you catch a cold? You need vitamins too, lots and lots of vitamins. I'm sure I heard that somewhere."

Samantha pulled Callum back, kissing him softly. "We need to get married first." She giggled as Callum merely nodded, looking dazed, panicked and more excited than she had ever seen him. Samantha turned to her brother, embraced him and let him rub her flat tummy, let him feel the two little beings growing inside her.

"Do you think Bella will be upset if I steal the priest for ten minutes to get married here before you two do the thing properly?" she asked hesitantly, not wanting to spoil Bella's immaculate plans.

"I think we can manage something."

* * * * *

Twenty minutes later, Samantha kissed Callum, tears once again in her eyes and her heart full of love as the priest pronounced them man and wife. For the first time ever, she felt Callum press her mind gently. She showed him her love, her happiness and her excitement over their babies.

Dimly, she heard her parents, siblings and family cheer happily for her and her brand-new husband. She pulled back from the kiss, slightly shy at such a huge public display.

She turned and caught her Uncle Dominic winking at her, his grin cheeky and cocky. Her Uncle Samuel stood next to him, smiling happily but poking Dominic every few seconds. Even over the cheers and well wishes she could hear Uncle Samuel telling Uncle Dominic to explain the secret he was obviously keeping.

Samantha turned to where Alexander stood with an arm protectively covering Bella. Curious about the change in plans earlier, Alex had sought Bella out. At first he had been distressed to see her unwell, but the discovery of impending fatherhood had nearly brought him to his knees with worry. As Samantha had guessed, her twin had indeed then turned utterly neurotic, and she was determined to enjoy every moment of teasing this would afford her. Bella had managed to calm him, but Samantha knew he would coddle her and cherish her every moment of the rest of their lives.

"You look much happier now, Mrs. MacLennon," a sexy voice whispered in her ear.

Samantha turned and smiled at her husband.

How she loved that word. *Husband.*

"I am feeling much happier now, Mr. MacLennon. Thank you for understanding," she added softly, still hoping he wouldn't regret letting her have a much smaller ceremony like she had wanted.

"Sammi," Callum replied huskily. "If you keep on looking at me like that we'll never make it to Bella and Alexander's wedding."

She smiled and took his hand, wanting to lead him back to the main house. Hugging and thanking her extended family for their well-wishes, they finally managed to get free and start the walk back.

"We have time," She cast him a hot glance, searing him and making herself damp. "More than enough time for a quickie."

"You're going to do this to me when we're old and gray and have grandkids fighting all around us, aren't you, darling?" he teased her softly, guiding her with one strong arm as the other clasped her hand in his.

"Certainly," she replied with no hesitation. "Someone has to keep you on your toes."

"I love you, Sammi."

Samantha stopped for a moment, bent in and kissed her husband firmly on his delicious mouth. Tugging his hand hard, she hurried them both back to the house. "I love you too, Callum. Let me show you just how much."

Also by Elizabeth Lapthorne

ഇ

eBooks:

Bonded for Eternity

Ellora's Cavemen: Legendary Tails I (*anthology*)

Hidden Desires

Kinkily Ever After

Lion in Love

Merc and Her Men

Montague Vampires: Desperate and Dateless

Montague Vampires: Flaming Fantasies

Montague Vampires: Heated Fantasies

Montague Vampires: Secret Fantasies

Payback

Urban Seductions 1: Retrieving Love

Urban Seductions 2: Retrieving Desire

Rutledge Werewolves 1: Scent of Passion

Rutledge Werewolves 2: Hide and Seek

Rutledge Werewolves 3: The Mating Game

Rutledge Werewolves 4: My Heart's Passion

Rutledge Werewolves 5: Chasing Love

Rutledge Werewolves 6: Twin Temptations

About the Author

∞

Elizabeth Lapthorne has been writing professionally since 2002. She has been astonished by the sucess of her Rutledge Werewolf series, and finds immense pleasure in hearing from her fans. To date she has more than ten books out, a few of those even in paperback.

Elizabeth regularly goes to the gym to chew over her ideas; many a book has begun or been worked through while cycling on the bikes. She also loves to read, eat chocolate and talk for hours with her friends. Elizabeth would love to hear from her fans, and checks her email religiously.

∞

The author welcomes comments from readers. You can find her website and email address on her author bio page at www.ellorascave.com.

Tell Us What You Think

We appreciate hearing reader opinions about our books. You can email us at Comments@EllorasCave.com.

Why an electronic book?

We live in the Information Age—an exciting time in the history of human civilization, in which technology rules supreme and continues to progress in leaps and bounds every minute of every day. For a multitude of reasons, more and more avid literary fans are opting to purchase e-books instead of paper books. The question from those not yet initiated into the world of electronic reading is simply: *Why?*

1. *Price.* An electronic title at Ellora's Cave Publishing runs anywhere from 40% to 75% less than the cover price of the exact same title in paperback format. Why? Basic mathematics and cost. It is less expensive to publish an e-book (no paper and printing, no warehousing and shipping) than it is to publish a paperback, so the savings are passed along to the consumer.

2. *Space.* Running out of room in your house for your books? That is one worry you will never have with electronic books. For a low one-time cost, you can purchase a handheld device specifically designed for e-reading. Many e-readers have large, convenient screens for viewing. Better yet, hundreds of titles can be stored within your new library—on a single microchip. There are a variety of e-readers from different manufacturers. You can also read e-books on your PC or laptop computer. (Please note that Ellora's Cave does not endorse any specific brands.

You can check our website at www.ellorascave.com for information we make available to new consumers.)

3. *Mobility.* Because your new e-library consists of only a microchip within a small, easily transportable e-reader, your entire cache of books can be taken with you wherever you go.

4. *Personal Viewing Preferences.* Are the words you are currently reading too small? Too large? Too... ANNOYING? Paperback books cannot be modified according to personal preferences, but e-books can.

5. *Instant Gratification.* Is it the middle of the night and all the bookstores near you are closed? Are you tired of waiting days, sometimes weeks, for bookstores to ship the novels you bought? Ellora's Cave Publishing sells instantaneous downloads twenty-four hours a day, seven days a week, every day of the year. Our webstore is never closed. Our e-book delivery system is 100% automated, meaning your order is filled as soon as you pay for it.

Those are a few of the top reasons why electronic books are replacing paperbacks for many avid readers.

As always, Ellora's Cave welcomes your questions and comments. We invite you to email us at Comments@ellorascave.com or write to us directly at Ellora's Cave Publishing Inc., 1056 Home Avenue, Akron, OH 44310-3502.

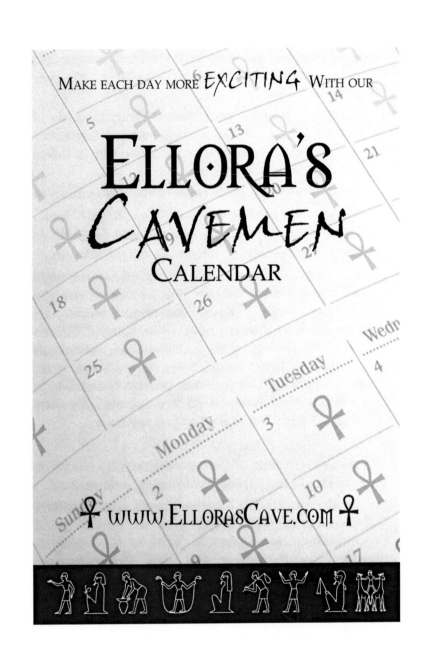

MAKE EACH DAY MORE *EXCITING* WITH OUR

ELLORA'S CAVEMEN

CALENDAR

www.EllorasCave.com

ELLORA'S CAVE
Romanticon

Annual convention
for women who
refuse to behave

Discover for yourself why readers can't get enough
of the multiple award-winning publisher

Ellora's Cave.

Whether you prefer e-books or paperbacks,

be sure to visit EC on the web at
www.ellorascave.com

for an erotic reading experience that will leave you
breathless.

CPSIA information can be obtained at www.ICGtesting.com
Printed in the USA
268549BV00001B/241/P

9 781419 964473